JACOB Z. FLORES

SPELL
FALL

Published by

DREAMSPINNER PRESS

5032 Capital Circle SW, Suite 2, PMB# 279, Tallahassee, FL 32305-7886 USA
www.dreamspinnerpress.com

Spell Fall
© 2017 Jacob Z. Flores.

Cover Art
© 2017 Paul Richmond.
http://www.paulrichmondstudio.com
Cover content is for illustrative purposes only and any person depicted on the cover is a model.

ISBN: 978-1-63533-215-5
Digital ISBN: 978-1-63533-216-2
Library of Congress Control Number: 2016915171
Published January 2017
v. 1.0

Printed in the United States of America
∞
This paper meets the requirements of
ANSI/NISO Z39.48-1992 (Permanence of Paper).

Readers love The Warlock Brothers of Havenbridge series by JACOB Z. FLORES

Spell Bound

"I loved this book It's hard to think of anything else to say. Read it. It's a wonderful mix of young love, magic, and true love. Also, I'm dying for book two."

—Joyfully Jay

"This was a wonderful read! I devoured it all in one day."

—Boys in our Books

Blood Tied

"The writing is supreme, the story is an intricately woven idea that intrigued me, brought me in from the beginning."

—On Top Down Under Book Reviews

"There was so much action and intrigue and I was on the edge of my seat the entire time."

—Prism Book Alliance

Soul Struck

"The third stunning installment in the fantastical Warlock Brothers of Havenbridge series, *Soul Struck* absolutely satisfies."

—Joyfully Reviewed

"This is such a rich and wonderful series. The world building is phenomenal and the characters each have their unique path to follow to become great warlocks and partners."

—The Blogger Girls

By Jacob Z. Flores

3
Being True
The Gifted One
Please Remember Me

DREAMSPUN DESIRES
ONE FINE DAY
#12 Undercover Boyfriend
#18 – Suddenly Yours

PROVINCETOWN
When Love Takes Over
Chasing the Sun
When Love Gets Hairy
When Love Comes to Town

THE WARLOCK BROTHERS OF HAVENBRIDGE
Spell Bound
Blood Tied
Soul Struck
Spell Fall

Published by Dreamspinner Press
www.dreamspinnerpress.com

To Lara.
This book wouldn't have been possible without you.
Thank you so much for your love, your kindness, your support,
and your time.

INTRODUCTION AND DRAMATIS PERSONAE

MAGIC HAS existed since the dawn of mankind. Its source is the Gate, a portal to the astral plane that powers the wonders of the world. From this Gate, a new species—the *homo magus*—evolved from humans and divided into three different subspecies: *homo ater magus*, or warlocks, *homo albus magus*, or witches, and *homo neuter magus*, or wizards.

From the moment humans first witnessed the power of this new species, the *homo magus* were hunted with extreme prejudice and brought to the brink of extinction.

But the *homo magus* survived by forming a secret society that lives amid humans.

The witch hunters still exist today, continuing their pursuit of eradicating magic. As long as they are hunted, warlocks, witches, and wizards will continue to live in secret, protecting themselves from extinction while saving humans from the new enemies and ancient threats they know nothing about.

THE BLACKMOORS (WARLOCKS)

Pierce Blackmoor is the oldest of his siblings and the future High Priest of his coven, a duty he now takes seriously. After suffering through a brief period in which his brothers possessed more power than he did, Pierce has increased his command over lightning. He can now see energy auras and transform his body into living lightning.

Thad Blackmoor is the middle child. He is coolly logical and often aloof. He uses his ice abilities to strategic advantage. His powers have grown as well. He can now create snow storms and call forth blizzards. Knowledge is far more important to Thad than defeating his enemies.

Mason Blackmoor is the youngest of his siblings. He initially had trouble controlling his magic and accessing his active power. Mason has since learned he is a shadow weaver, which means he can bend the darkness to his will. This is a rare and powerful warlock ability that has led to the corruption of every warlock who has ever wielded it.

Drake Carpenter, a human and Mason's boyfriend, has been made an honorary member of the Blackmoor coven. His last surviving relative, Aunt Millie, was murdered by a vampyre. Drake is under the protection of the Blackmoors due to his part in the death of the vampyre who killed his aunt and because of his uncanny immunity to magic, which has made him invaluable against vengeful shadow weavers and psychotic sorcerers.

Aiden Teine joined the Blackmoor family after being cast out of Otherworld, the land of the fairies, when he was turned into the first vampyre fae. As a fire fae and former prince of his realm, Aiden struggles with balancing his conflicting fae and vampyren tendencies. His love for Thad continues to keep his more dangerous instincts at bay.

Kale Aquilo is a shifter and the most recent addition to the Blackmoor family. When he first arrived from the shifters' magically shrouded island, Aeaea, Kale was as timid and docile as the dove he turned into. However, his love for Pierce and the devastation brought to his home by shadow weaver Ben Crane and the mad sorcerer Sersie gave Kale the ability to transform into an eagle. Kale now serves as the chief advisor to the Beast King and as a liaison between his people and the rest of the magical community.

Oliver Blackmoor is the head of his family and the High Priest of his coven. Although many still consider him the most powerful warlock in the family, since he can turn his entire body into stone, his sons' growing magical abilities have begun to eclipse his own. He is often distant and irritable, but Oliver loves his sons and his ever-growing family. He also still grieves for his wife.

Priscilla Blackmoor was Oliver's wife and mother to Pierce, Thad, and Mason. She died from breast cancer one year ago.

THE PROCTORS (WITCHES)

Charles and Camille Proctor are the High Priests of their coven. Charles, who works for the Havenbridge Police Department as a detective, is capable of commanding fire, while Camille has dominion over plants. The Proctors pride themselves on the white magic they practice, which connects them to the spiritual forces of the universe.

Adam Proctor is the oldest of his siblings and the future High Priest of his coven. His guiding element of magic is air, which allows him to use it offensively or defensively. Adam's rocky past with Pierce Blackmoor has been resolved, and he no longer nurses his previous wounds for the unrequited feelings he once had for Mason.

Charlotte Proctor finds herself bookended by two strong-willed siblings. She is the peacemaker in the family, and this characteristic manifests in her powers. Charlotte taps into the element of water, which grants her astounding healing abilities. She is also a staunch supporter of the Conclave.

Miranda Proctor fancies herself the rebel in her family. She is loud and opinionated, which often gets her in trouble and sets her at odds with her family. This explains why Miranda and Mason Blackmoor do not get along; they are two peas in a pod. Miranda's active power derives from the spirit element, which grants her a unique ability to teleport objects and people at will.

THE STONEWALLS (WIZARDS)

Lawrence and Rachel Stonewall are the High Priests of their coven. The gray magic of wizards gives them direct access to the spirit element, which allows them to tap into powerful abilities that are kept in check by their logical ways. Lawrence is able to control minds while Rachel can cast illusions.

Edith Stonewall is the eldest of her siblings. She is the future High Priest of her coven and can erect invisible force fields for protection. She is also the most like her parents. She rarely engages with others outside her coven, although she does share a friendship with Pierce. She is closest, however, with her twin brother, Elliot.

Elliot Stonewall is Edith's twin brother, younger by three minutes. He is mute and cannot access his magic like others in the community. He does, however, have the ability to speak to others telepathically.

Kate and Keaton Stonewall are the youngest members of the family, and they are also twins. Neither has tapped into their active powers because they are still too young. Once they turn sixteen, they will learn what ability they will have at their disposal.

OTHER CHARACTERS

The Conclave is the governing body of the magical community. The three most powerful warlocks, witches, and wizards serve on the

Conclave. They are charged with making and enforcing magical laws as well as ensuring the Gate is protected from all threats. The word of the Conclave is absolute, and their power is feared across the magical community. Currently, the Conclave and the Blackmoors are at odds.

Gerald Wa, a wizard and the only identified member of the Conclave, acts as an advisor to the protector covens. He was believed to be dead, but his death was staged to hide his ascension to the Conclave. Prior to this "death," Gerald was romantically involved with Drake's aunt Millie. The information Gerald provides to the protector covens and more specifically to the Blackmoors used to place him at odds with the rest of the governing body. However, Gerald and the Blackmoors have had a falling out, and the current nature of their relationship is unknown.

The Warlock Hag is a member of the Conclave. Although her identity is unknown, she has made her dislike of the Blackmoors evident. Her animosity toward the Blackmoors places her and Gerald at odds, especially since she wants to replace the Blackmoors with the Edwells as the protector coven for the Order of the Black.

The Edwells consist of Leopold and Agnes and their teenage daughter, Charity. Although the Proctors and the Stonewalls do not like them, they put up with their presence. The Blackmoors, however, display open hostility for the coven they consider to be made of opportunistic weasels.

Sersie was a sorcerer, a magical species that resulted from humans and magical beings interbreeding. In 700 BC, Sersie led a rebellion, along with other sorcerers, against the magical community. She cast a spell that turned humans into the first shifters. To escape death at the conclusion of the Sorcerer Wars, Sersie transformed her soul into a wraith. With the help of Ben Crane, Sersie possessed the body of a young sorcerer named Chloe and came back to exact her revenge until she was killed by Pierce.

Bartram Kane lived during the Salem Witch Trials. Bartram was a powerful member of the Conclave of his time. He was also the last warlock to possess the abilities of a shadow weaver. When his son Ebenezer was burned at the stake, Bartram went mad. He spoke the forbidden *immortalitas* spell to resurrect his son but turned him into a vampyre instead.

Ebenezer Kane/Ben Crane came back to life as a vampyre after his father spoke the *immortalitas* spell. Ebenezer created other vampyren and almost destroyed the magical and human communities. The Conclave needed its combined might to stop him. During the present day, Ebenezer took on the identity of Ben Crane and decimated Otherworld, the land of the fae, and Aeaea, the shifters' magical island. He stole two of the Crests of the Five, which are physical manifestations of the five mystical elements, for someone identified as Ica, the individual truly pulling Ebenezer's strings. Pierce killed Ben during his attempt to steal the third crest within the crown of the Beast King.

Ica is the unknown enemy the Blackmoors and the rest of the protector covens have been fighting. His true name and the motives behind his pursuit of the Crests of the Five remain a mystery to all except the Conclave.

CHAPTER 1

"ARE YOU okay, Drake?"

No, I wasn't okay. In fact, I was about as far away from being okay as you could possibly get, but my throat kept me from answering. I glanced into the face and eyes of the boy I loved. Mason shook the strands of hair away from his face, but he couldn't shake away the sadness that flooded his gaze. It told me he'd do anything to take away my pain.

If only grief could be spirited away so easily.

I swallowed hard, trying to force my throat open to respond, but the emotions that bubbled up from my soul refused to budge. They sat there, waiting for the moment when my resolve fell and the pain ripping me to pieces inside came flooding out.

Mason moved to stand behind me and wrapped his arms around my chest, holding me tight. I inhaled his musky, sweet scent and embraced the warmth of his touch and the soothing rhythm of his heartbeat. His love and devotion prevented me from being swept away by the pain I'd yet to fully express.

It told me that I didn't have to talk. All I had to do was be held.

I leaned into his touch, drawing on the strength he always gave me, and returned my attention to the sturdy half Cape house surrounded by the white picket fence. I could still see my aunt Millie tending to the garden and fussing at me for helping her. God, how she hated that! She would always tell me she could do it her damn self, and despite her advanced age, painful arthritis, and heart arrhythmia, she meant every word. She was the definition of an independent woman with a spirit stronger than a wild mustang running across the prairie, and this house had been her pride and joy.

It was also where she had been murdered, where magic stole something dear from me, and where my aunt Millie had been turned into a vampyre. My heart sank.

"I miss her somethin' awful." The white plumes of vapor that exited my body in short, rapid spurts told me it was cold, but I couldn't feel the sharp sting of the chilly air. I had been numb ever since I woke up that morning because I knew that today I'd be saying one final good-bye to the house that had been my home for too brief a time.

Mason held me tighter, rubbing his cheek against mine. It always made me feel safe when he did that. It told me he was here for whatever I needed. He'd been there for me ever since we met, even if we didn't particularly like each other at first.

He had protected me, saved me, loved me, and given the boy who had lost his entire world a new family.

"I miss her too. She was the best."

I nodded, tears streaming down my cheeks. She was the best of the best, and this world was a sadder place now that the monster Ben Crane had turned her into had replaced the Millicent Carpenter I knew. The five-foot-three woman with a heart of gold and a soul of steel was gone. Only a seven-foot-tall vampyre with jagged teeth and a prehensile tongue remained, and the woman who once did everything she could to protect me now tried to kill me every time our paths crossed.

And I was likely going to have to run a stake through her heart.

"I don't know if I can do this."

"You don't have to." Mason turned me around in his arms and pressed his forehead to mine in a show of solidarity. "You can back out of the sale. You know my dad would take care of it."

I had no doubt. Oliver Blackmoor had taken care of so much for me already. Besides welcoming me into his home and his family with open arms, he had been the one to hire the realtor, to make sure the house was ready for the market, and ultimately the one who had negotiated the sale. For an intimidating warlock who could turn his body into stone, he was one of the sweetest men in the world. I couldn't have asked for a better surrogate father.

"No. It's time to say good-bye." I glanced over my shoulder, sweeping my gaze across the house and the garden as the sun slowly sank behind the roofline. "It just seems so final. Like I'm givin' up on savin' Aunt Millie."

Mason didn't respond. He knew exactly what I wanted, what I had been poring through all the magical texts in the Blackmoor library to find—a spell that would release my aunt from the vampyren curse and return her to the woman she'd once been.

Thad, Mason's older brother, the one the family teasingly called Brainiac, had told me on countless occasions that no such magic existed, that the *immortalitas* spell could not be broken. In the months since Aunt Millie had been turned, I had refused to accept that, and no one had tried to make me, but now, well, now that the house had been sold, I couldn't help but feel as if I had failed.

"Drake, I want you to listen to me. Okay?"

I returned my gaze to his and nodded.

"You're not giving up because I'm not giving up. We'll keep looking, and one of these days we *will* find something."

Tears tumbled down my cheeks as I smiled up at him. How had I been so lucky to fall in love with the sweetest, most handsome warlock ever born? "You really think so?"

He pressed his lips to mine. "I know so."

Mason's words refilled my soul with the strength it thrived on. I had spent too many hours recently wallowing in grief and dread. It was time to let hope and determination back in. That was the son my parents had raised. That was the type of person Aunt Millie had been every day of her life. That was the type of person I had to be, the Drake Carpenter who honored the memory of his lost loved ones not with tears and misery but with happiness and vigor.

I wrapped my arms around Mason's neck and drew his lips to mine. "Thank you."

"For what?"

"For bein' you."

A devious smirk twisted his lips. "You usually get upset when I'm being me."

He had me there. While I might be crazy in love with Mason, sometimes he just drove me crazy. "This you I approve of."

Mason snuffed. "What happened to love being unconditional?"

"Oh, it's conditional, all right. Definitely conditional."

"Well, that's not very romantic." The fake scowl on his face almost made me laugh. No matter how bad things got or how shattered I felt, I could always count on him to make me feel better.

"There's just one condition."

He blew the strands of hair from his eyes. "And what's that?"

"That you love me forever."

Mason's smile lit up his face. "Only if you promise to love me forever."

"Easiest promise ever."

"Good, then it's se—" Mason froze as his gaze darted over my shoulder.

"What is it?"

He grabbed me and shoved me toward the car. "Get in and don't come out until I tell you to."

"What the hell is goin' on?" I wheeled around and glanced into the street-facing windows of the cottage. When I saw who was staring back at me, I gasped.

It was Aunt Millie.

I WATCHED in horror as Mason ran up the sidewalk and sprinted for the front door. He couldn't go in there, especially not alone. Aunt Millie would kill him. "Mason, no!"

"Get in the car," he yelled over his shoulder as he bounded up the porch steps.

Like hell I was. "Wait for me."

He spun around and gestured at me. "*Remane.*"

In response, my legs suddenly wouldn't work, no matter how hard I willed them to start running. Damn him! I was immune to all magic but Mason's. No one knew why other people's spells had no effect on me if I didn't want them to, but Thad had a theory about why Mason's did. We were spell bound, two souls that had been connected across several past lives. That magical connection allowed Mason's spells to work on me, to protect me, because our love gave him as much power over me as I had over him.

"Don't you go in there!"

Mason blew me a kiss before shoving open the door and disappearing inside.

Of all the irresponsible, hotheaded things he could do, this was by far the stupidest move Mason had ever made. He was going after a vampyre, a creature who not only built up immunity to spells but who could kill him without half trying, alone. If he made it out of this alive, I was going to kill him.

Somehow I had to get in there and help him, but I had to call in reinforcements first. I pulled my phone out of my pocket.

Aunt Millie is here. At her house. Come quick!

After I hit Send, I shoved my phone back into my pocket and focused on my legs. My brain screamed at them to run, to get to Mason before Aunt Millie did, but they wouldn't respond. While I was glad Mason's power was growing stronger every day, right now the power of his spell pissed me off.

I had to get to him, and no one, not even Mason, was going to get in my way.

I let out a cry of fury and pain, using all the willpower I could muster to move. My thigh muscles shook and spasmed as I tried to force my legs free. Sweat dripped down my face in tiny rivulets. It was like I was working out in the middle of summer instead of being deep in a Massachusetts winter.

My right foot rose an inch off the snow-covered sidewalk before the remnants of Mason's spell forced it back down. It was working. My immunity to magic was counteracting the spell. All I had to do was give it one final push and I'd be free to run after Mason, help him fight Aunt Millie, and then kick his ass all the way back home.

I took a deep breath and put all my strength into my next attempt. With one final howl, I managed to tear my right leg free of Mason's spell, and a second later I was dashing down the sidewalk and through the front door.

I tried the lights, but they weren't working. I wasn't surprised. They hadn't been working the last time a vampyre had been sneaking around inside. Since the sun had set, I could only see a few feet into the living room. All I could make out was an empty room.

No Mason. No Aunt Millie.

"Mason!"

No response either.

I inched forward, stopping where the light cast by the lampposts outside ended and the inky darkness of the room began. Once I crossed the threshold, there would be no turning back. I would be alone, in the dark, with a woman I loved dearly who wanted to kill the boy I loved, rip open my throat, and drink my blood.

"Mason!" I screamed at the top of my lungs. I scanned the shadows, searching for movement and listening for the telltale hiss of a vampyre ready to attack.

There was only silence.

If Mason were okay, he'd be telling me to quit yelling and get in there. He'd be bitching that he couldn't stop Aunt Millie before she flew off into the evening sky. He'd also be complaining that I should have listened and waited for him in his car.

But he wasn't doing any of those things, which meant I had to do what I feared the most: enter the darkness, face my aunt Millie, and do whatever I had to, to make sure she didn't hurt Mason.

I took a deep breath and stepped out of the light and into the shadows.

No one suddenly rushed me, so I inched farther into the room, putting more distance between myself and the door that led to safety. I scanned the dark interior, my eyes sweeping past the barren walls where my aunt Millie's collection of floral prints once hung. I moved past the place where her light green couch once sat, the spot where she worked on the *New York Times* crossword while she watched *Jeopardy!* I plunged farther into the house that had once been my refuge, and with each step, my heartbeat thundered in my ears and my breath grew more and more ragged.

My phone chimed and I practically jumped out of my skin. It was most likely Thad finally responding. He was probably telling me to get the hell out of here, to run as fast as I could, to not go inside the house. I couldn't tell him it was too late. If I opened my phone and stared into the bright screen, it would momentarily blind me. I couldn't afford any disadvantage right now because no matter how much I loved my aunt Millie, she would kill me at the first opportunity.

I had to be prepared. I had to keep going. I had to save Mason if he wasn't already—

No. I couldn't go there.

I pressed my back against the living room wall that stood adjacent to the entrance to the kitchen. From here, the shadowed hallway that led to the bedrooms opened like a dark mouth to my left, while the shadowy kitchen lay to my right. If I went into the hallway, I'd give the shadows in the kitchen my back. If I went into the kitchen, whatever waited for me in the hallway would be able to reach out and devour me whole.

I had to make a choice, and I had to make it fast.

After a quick glance into the maw of the hallway, I sprinted into the kitchen. The only things that greeted me were the stainless-steel appliances Aunt Millie regularly polished. In the uncertain light, they glinted like apparitions. I darted for the back door and looked out the window onto the garden in the backyard I used to tend for her. No one stood on the frozen, dead ground that had once been filled with hydrangeas, chrysanthemums, and calla lilies. As I swept my gaze across the entire width of the property, the memory of Mason's first visit played in my mind.

He had cast a spell that brought a storm of butterflies fluttering around us while I'd been planting. Aunt Millie had such a big smile on her face that day. She'd never seen so many butterflies in her life, and she had giggled like a schoolgirl when they alighted in her hair. That was the Aunt Millie I'd always remember, the independent woman who lived life on her terms and embraced every moment with childlike wonder.

"Drake?"

I spun around, expecting to find my aunt Millie standing behind me, but there was only darkness. How was that possible? Her voice had been barely a whisper. She could be nowhere else but in this room with me.

"Drake, honey. Can you hear me?" Her voice floated on the air like a ghost.

I walked a circle around the small kitchen, cutting my gaze into the shadowy alcove behind the stacked washer and dryer, over to the breakfast nook where we used to eat cereal together, and back to the sink. Where the heck was she?

"I'm over here, you silly boy."

I froze and glanced down at the kitchen sink.

"Aunt Millie?" I muttered, leaning over the drain.

"There you are." Her voice was sweeter than syrup, and it freaked me out.

I knew exactly where she was now. I took a step back and crouched before the cabinet under the sink. I carefully opened the door. Beyond the small removable shelf sat a ledge that overlooked the basement below the house. When I first discovered this bizarre part of the house shortly after moving in, Aunt Millie explained that the house was designed this way to keep the basement, where the furnace was located, ventilated while the house was warmed during the winter.

The gaping, black hole had reminded me of something out of a horror novel back then. It terrified me even more right now.

"Come down here for a minute, will you? I need your help."

I shook my head and crawled backward like a crab. There was no way in hell I was going down there.

"By the way, are you and Mason staying for dinner?"

The cruel mocking in her question bit deep. She knew how terrified I was of the basement, but she also knew I wouldn't be able to run away. Mason was down there with her, and if I didn't do as she requested, she'd kill him without a second thought.

I crawled back over to the cabinet and removed the shelf, exposing the small landing that opened up into an endless void. From what I remembered, the drop was only a few feet, and the steps leading up to the outside entrance were about seven feet to the right. If I needed a speedy exit, I was going to have to rely on my memory to get me up the staircase and out the door.

Before I climbed into the small space, I took my phone out of my pocket and placed it in front of the open cabinet doors. It was the only clue I could think of to leave Thad so he and the others would know where to find me—just in case.

I went in to the cabinet feetfirst, sending them dangling into the dark ocean. When I was perched on the ledge, half in the kitchen and half in the basement, I gave myself one final push before falling into the darkness.

I LANDED with a huff and immediately stood up, waiting to feel the sting of claws against my flesh or the tight grip of Aunt Millie's prehensile tongue wrap around my throat. Again, nothing happened. When I had encountered her on our way to Otherworld and on Aeaea, she didn't hesitate to try to kill me. What the hell was she waiting for now?

I took a deep breath, trying to calm the tremor in my voice. "Aunt Millie?"

"Well, what are you waiting for? An invitation? Turn on the light so you can give me a hand."

I reached up into the void, feeling for the string that would dispel the darkness. When my searching fingers finally found it, I pulled.

I shielded my eyes as they adjusted to the sudden light. I could only make out boxes that lined the walls of the room, but after a few moments, I spotted Mason lying on his back in the middle of the basement.

I rushed to his side and crouched next to him. He had a pulse, and his throat was still intact. She hadn't killed him, but why?

"It seems like forever since I last laid eyes on you."

I spun around to find Aunt Millie standing in front of the steps that led out of the basement. She wasn't in her vampyren form, with six-inch claws extending from her fingertips. No snakelike tongue rattled out of her mouth, which was usually lined with razor-sharp teeth. Her hair was gray, not silver and ratted, and it was held back by two brown barrettes that matched the caramel hue of the wizened eyes that gave me strength every day after my parents died. She looked upon me like she always had, with love, not murder.

This didn't make sense. From what Thad had told me, humans who had been turned into vampyren couldn't control their transformation. Once someone became a vampyre, they stayed a vampyre. Only magical beings like Ben and Aiden could move between the two forms. If that was true, how was Aunt Millie in her human form right now?

"How is this possible?" I motioned to her. "How are you, well, *you*?"

She glanced down at herself and smiled as if she was wearing an evening dress. "It's wonderful, isn't it?"

Tears welled up in my eyes. I wanted nothing more than to run into her arms and bury my face in her neck like I did on the day she arrived in Dallas to bring me to Havenbridge. "Yes, it is." I forced the words past the sob in my throat. "But how?"

"It happened shortly after Ebenezer was vanquished on Aeaea. I suddenly felt more like myself again. Perhaps it was because he was my sire, and since he was dead, well, whatever influence he'd been exerting over me just went"—she wiggled her fingers as if she were casting a spell—"poof!"

I guess that made some sense. A lot about vampyren was still unknown because they were too unstable and too bloodthirsty to study.

"As I'm sure you probably guessed," she continued, "I hated being controlled by that man—warlock, vampyre, *whatever* you want to call him. I didn't enjoy answering to *anyone* when I was alive, so you can be damn sure I didn't get a real kick out of taking orders as one of the undead."

I tilted my head to one side and studied her. She was talking as if nothing had changed, as if she were still the same Millicent Carpenter she was before Ben sank his teeth into her. What was her game?

"So I must apologize for trying to kill you all those times. I hope you can forgive me." She clasped her hands under her chin and locked gazes with me. When I didn't answer, her brown eyes turned cross the way they used to whenever I pushed the limits of her patience. "Has the cat got a hold of your tongue again?"

"Yes, ma'am. I'm sorry about that."

"So can you? Forgive me?"

"Sure." Where was this particular bend in the road taking us?

A grin spread across her wrinkled face as she took two steps toward me. I took two steps back. She let out a sigh and nodded. "I guess this is as close as we are going to get, isn't it?" She laced her fingers together and rested them against her chest.

"It's probably for the best."

She thought about it for a few seconds before giving me a reluctant nod. "Yes, you're probably right. I might not want to kill you right now, but things could change."

I gulped. "What are you doin' here?"

She snorted. "This is my house."

"But you're—"

"Dead. Yes, I know, but that doesn't change the fact that this is *still* my house."

I wasn't going to argue ownership with her. That would only make her angry, and upsetting a vampyre in a room with the only accessible exit blocked wasn't the wisest move. What I had to do was keep her distracted and talking. That would give the Blackmoors time to get here. While I might be immune to magic, I couldn't go against a vampyre's claws and teeth without a stake in my hand.

"Okay, so *why* are you here?"

"Because of you."

I swallowed hard. "Are you here to kill me?"

A smile hitched up the left corner of her lips. "No, dear. If I was, you'd be dead by now and so would Mason." She gazed down at my unconscious boyfriend and took a deep breath.

"So why, then?"

"You've been thrown into a dangerous world, Drake. One that holds more surprises than you are even aware of."

"What do you mean?"

She shook her head. "I can't say. Just like the human world, this world comes with its own set of rules. If I were to tell you what I know in an attempt to steer you from a certain path, I could inadvertently steer you in the direction I don't want you to go."

"Then why are you here if you can't tell me anythin'?"

She smiled at me as if she was looking at the most precious thing in her world, and I had to once again fight the desire to fly into her arms. "Because I love you, Drake. That never stopped. Not the moment I died and not after I'd been turned. I only did what I did because I had no other choice."

Was that true? Had my aunt lived inside the monster this whole time? If so, that meant I was right all along. She *could* be saved. All I had to do was find the right spell that would set her free.

Before I had time to think, I rushed over to her and took her hands in mine. "We can fix this, Aunt Millie. The Blackmoors are powerful warlocks. They have access to some of the strongest spells in existence. There has to be some way to break the vampyren curse."

She slid her hands from mine, caressed my cheeks, and smiled. "There is a way, Drake, and I'm hoping you will help me."

I placed my hands over hers and nodded. "I'll do anythin'."

"I'm hoping that's true." She let my cheeks go and turned around, grabbing something off the shelf behind her. When she faced me again, she placed a wooden stake in my hand and wrapped my fingers around it.

I dropped it immediately and backed away. "No. I won't do it!"

"You must." She bent down to pick it back up in one fluid motion. The arthritis she suffered in life had clearly disappeared in death. "Before it's too late."

I didn't understand. She'd been released from Ben's control after Pierce killed him. "But it's not too late. You're free. You're *you* again."

"For the moment, yes." The love in her eyes was strong, and it made my soul soar. "But a new enemy rises. When this being comes into power, my mind will no longer be mine."

Who the heck was she talking about? "Do you mean Ica?"

"The name is Icarian." The words came out with a mixture of awe and loathing.

"If you can tell me Icarian's name or that he's risin' to power, why can't you tell me everythin' else?"

She looked at me as if I was a seven-year-old requesting ice cream and cake for dinner. "You learned about Icarian on Aeaea, and you and the Blackmoors have pieced together parts of the plan." How did she know all this? Had she been watching me since Ben's death? "I can tell you these things because you already know them. It's what you don't know that I can't discuss."

"Well, I don't care about Icarian or these stupid rules. I care about you, and I can't do what you're askin' me to do."

"If you don't, you doom me to this." The kind, loving woman who took me in suddenly disappeared, replaced by a seven-foot-tall monster with gnashing teeth and razor claws. Her tongue shot from between her fangs, snaking in the air as if it were searching for a feast. "I will try to kill you. I can feel the urge to drink your blood consuming every ounce of will I have remaining. It's too hard to fight."

I backed away. "Then shift back. Now!"

"No," she hissed, tossing the stake over to me. She hid behind her claws as if she couldn't bear to face me. "This is the only way to end it."

"Drake!" Mr. Blackmoor's frantic voice yelled from upstairs. "Where are you?"

"I'm down here in the basement. Hurry!" I dropped the stake again and met my aunt's murderous gaze. "I won't!"

"You will!" Aunt Millie bellowed as footsteps thundered overhead. In less than a second, she wrapped her tongue around Mason's throat, causing his carotid artery to bulge under the skin. She raised her hand, ready to deliver the blow that would kill the boy I loved, before glancing over her shoulder at me. Her tongue retracted as her claws hovered inches above his flesh. "I will kill Mason and his family. Then I will kill you." She trembled, except this time it wasn't out of bloodlust. The cold, dead vampyren eyes had reverted back to the kind brown of the woman I loved and admired, and that woman was terrified. Her gaze begged me to end her pain. "Let me march into the Gate on my own terms, as the woman who loves you and not this monster."

My already broken heart shattered even further. This wasn't how it was supposed to be. I was supposed to find a spell to free Aunt Millie, not be the reason she died, but how could I argue with her? This was what she wanted. If our situations were reversed, I'd want the same thing.

A howl mixed with fury and soul-shredding pain tore from my chest. I picked up the stake, rushed toward her, and plunged it into her chest and through her heart.

Aunt Millie shrieked as she fell backward. Black blood bubbled out of the wound and between her fingers. I sat next to her, pulling her dying body onto my lap. Tears streamed down my face as I held her close.

"Don't cry." She rubbed the wetness from my cheeks before reverting to the woman I loved. "You saved me. That means you have what it takes to save us all."

I didn't know what she was talking about, and right then, I didn't care. All that mattered to me was that I was losing Aunt Millie once again.

"Oh my God, Drake!"

I glanced up to find Thad standing in the basement. Aiden, his fire fairy boyfriend, Pierce, and Mr. Blackmoor stood next to him. They gazed briefly at my aunt before settling their somber stares upon me.

"Do somethin'. Help me save her. Please." My voice broke and dropped to a tortured whisper. "I don't want to be alone again."

Mr. Blackmoor inched toward me and rested his hand on my shoulder.

"You're not alone." Aunt Millie cast her eyes on Mason. "You have each other." She flashed me a big, beautiful smile before a grimace stole it away. Her body was withering, slowly turning to ash. "But you both must be careful. The past returns to haunt your present."

"What are you talkin' about?" I asked through my tears. "What past?"

But she couldn't answer. Aunt Millie gave me one final smile before all that was left of her was a pile of dust.

CHAPTER 2

I COULDN'T get out of Aunt Millie's house fast enough. It took every ounce of strength I had not to fall apart after what I'd done.

How could I have killed her? Why didn't I insist we go back to the Blackmoors' and find a spell that would either revert her to her human form permanently or protect her from Icarian's influence? There had to be some other solution besides a stake.

My gut wrenched, and the sobs I'd been holding back broke through the dam.

Mason, whom Mr. Blackmoor had healed with a quick spell, stopped the car on the shoulder and pulled me into his arms. I fell into the crook of his neck, letting loose the waves of despair that continued to pound the shore of my soul.

"I've got you," he whispered before kissing the top of my head. "I always will."

I clung to those words more than ever. Mason was all I had left in this world now, and I'd do whatever was necessary to hang on to him.

He ran his fingers through my hair and brushed his lips across my forehead. "I'm sorry you had to do that to save me."

I pulled out of the embrace and shook my head. Mason couldn't go on thinking he had anything to do with what happened. I took several deep breaths and wiped the tears and snot from my face. "It's what she wanted." My voice cracked. "I had to."

"It shouldn't have been you."

Mason was wrong. If it had to be done, it was only right that I was the one to do it. "No. She was *my* aunt. After everythin' she did for me, settin' her free was the least I could do for her."

The stinging pain didn't bite as deeply after those words left my mouth. Sure, it still stung worse than a rattlesnake bite to the nuts, but I hadn't failed Aunt Millie. Who knew how long it would have been before I found a magical answer to her problem? It might have been weeks, months, even years, and in that time, she might have been forced to attack me again or kill more innocent people. She didn't want that, and I didn't want that for her.

Whether I liked it or not, whether it was fair or not, Aunt Millie was finally at peace.

As for where I went from here, well, it was time to put an end to this once and for all. The only way we were going to do that was if we found Icarian, put a stop to his plans, and made him pay.

"Your mood's changed." Mason lifted my chin with his thumb and forefinger and gazed deep into my eyes. "You look pissed."

"I am." My voice deepened, and the tears in my eyes dried. "I'm tired of sittin' and waitin', Mason. It's time we did somethin' about Icarian."

He nodded and put the car in drive.

Twenty minutes later Mason and I walked through the front door of Blackmoor Manor and made our way to the living room, where the family patiently waited for us.

Aiden sprinted to my side first and gobbled me up in the biggest bear hug of my life. I always forgot how strong he was, physically and magically. Even though he was six feet four inches of pure muscle, he always exuded a tenderness that dwarfed his frame and the power he wielded as the only vampyre fae in existence. His dual nature also gave him unique understanding of my turmoil. When Aiden had first been turned, thoughts of killing Thad practically drove him crazy. He had wanted to die too. Fortunately his fae side allowed him to gain control over his vampyren urges in a way that my human aunt Millie never could.

"I'm so sorry." He set me back down on the floor, his big green eyes hooded with grief. "You must be—"

"Numb." That was certainly a good word right now.

He half nodded, as if that wasn't quite right, and he would know. One of his fire fairy abilities happened to be reading emotions, and I had no doubt those prying fairy eyes of his were telling him a lot. "Yet I sense peace as well."

As surprising as that was, he was right. Knowing my aunt had crossed over to a better place settled the churning waters in my soul, but so did the emotion that filled the room. The usually calm and collected Thad stood behind Aiden, his shoulders slumped and his hazel eyes wet with tears. Worry tracked clear lines of concern across Pierce's usually snarling face. Mason's oldest brother typically responded to unpleasantness with fury and displays of power. Right now Pierce's red nose and puffy eyes told me his heart was breaking for me, and I loved him for that.

They grieved for my loss as they still grieved the loss of their mother.

"What can I do?" Mr. Blackmoor stood before me, resting his hands on my shoulders. Tears freely flowed down his big, bearded face, and he made no attempt to hide them or wipe them away.

He loved me not because I was in love with his son. He loved me because I had become one of his sons. "What you always do. Love and support me." I peered past Mr. Blackmoor to Pierce and Thad. "The way y'all have always done."

Mr. Blackmoor cleared the sob from his throat and nodded. "Yes. That's what a family does for each other."

"Damn straight," Pierce said with a sniffle and a smile.

Thad stood tall and nodded. "And it's what we'll always do."

I sucked back the tears that had welled up in my eyes. The time for crying had passed. It was time to act. "We need to discuss what happened with Aunt Millie."

"Are you sure?" Mr. Blackmoor surveyed the room. Most everyone else shook their heads, likely believing I needed sleep more than anything else. "It can wait 'til morning."

We had waited long enough. I owed it to my aunt to make sure that anyone who was responsible for what had happened to her paid the price. "No. It can't."

After they reluctantly nodded, I filled everyone in on what happened in the basement.

"She was in control of herself?" Thad's mouth was wide enough to shoot a basketball through. He'd come in after it was all over. He hadn't seen her walking around as Aunt Millie the person instead of Aunt Millie the vampyre. "I didn't think that was possible for humans."

"Neither did I." Mr. Blackmoor turned in his seat to Aiden, who stood sentry by Thad. "Aiden, what do you think? You're the only other vampyre we've known besides Ben who was capable of reverting to your non-vampyren form."

Aiden chewed it over for a few moments. "I suppose it's possible. I was able to revert back to my fae form after I'd been infected with the curse, but only because of Thad." When he gazed over at Thad, his emerald eyes sparkled. "Your love made it possible. You refused to give up on me even though all I wanted was to kill you and drink your blood."

Thad beamed up at him.

Pierce sat down next to his father, averting his eyes from Thad and Aiden's displays of affection. The old Pierce would have grimaced and told them to get a room, but since Pierce had fallen in love with a shifter named Kale, watching others happy in love no longer grossed him out. The droop in his eyes told us how much he missed Kale and counted down the days until he would return from his magically shrouded island. "If love made it possible for Aiden to gain control over his vampyren form, then your aunt's love for you could have done the same for her."

"But what does any of this have to do with stopping Icarian?" Mason asked.

"A lot, actually." Thad flipped through the Grimoire that contained the family's collection of spells. "If Aunt Millie was capable of controlling herself instead of bending to a more powerful magical will, then Icarian isn't at full power yet and can be stopped. That will be easier now that we know his real name."

Mason's dark eyebrows pinched together. "Why does that matter?"

"I know the answer to that one." Pierce jutted out his chin. Since defeating Ben and Sersie on Aeaea, he'd spent just as much time studying magic as Thad did. He was finally taking his role as the next High Priest of this coven seriously. "It has to do with names containing power, right?"

A huge smile spread across Thad's thin lips. "Exactly. Our attempts to find him since our time in Aeaea have failed because we believed his name to be Ica. That was why our magic wouldn't work. But now that we know his true name, we might be able to find a spell strong enough to locate him."

"And stop the Spell Fall?" Aiden's question made everyone pause.

We still had no clue what the Spell Fall even was. The Conclave hadn't taken the time to fill us in after they abandoned us on Shifter Island. They were too busy throwing a hissy fit because we had kept secrets from them even though they never shared any of theirs with us.

"We can certainly hope so." Mr. Blackmoor turned in his seat to face me. "But what about the rest of what your aunt Millie told you? What do you think she meant about your past coming back to haunt you?"

I had no clue. My parents were dead and so was Aunt Millie. I had no connections, no past with anyone before Havenbridge.

I STOOD in front of the living room window, scanning the expansive backyard, as if the winter landscape might somehow hold the answers. I found nothing amid the thick, white blanket of snow that covered the ground and stretched back toward the darkened woods on the outskirts of the property. No sudden revelation wafted on the gust of wind that kicked up a spray of snow and sent it barreling into the rattling limbs of the barren trees.

But the answer was out there. I could feel it skulking in the shadows, making its way to me, and the tightness in my chest told me I had to find it before it found me. That was why Aunt Millie had come to see me. She knew the danger. She wanted me to be ready, but she also needed to know if I could handle it. Was that part of the reason she wanted me to bring her existence as a vampyre to an end? Had it been a test?

One of the last things she told me wafted up from my memory. *"You have what it takes to save us all."*

Who was I saving, and what exactly was I saving them from?

"It's okay. We'll figure it out."

Mason's words made me flinch.

"Sorry." He encircled me in his arms and pulled me close. "I didn't mean to scare you."

"I know. I guess I'm just a little jumpy."

"That's not surprising, considering everything you've been through."

We had all been through a lot these past few months, and it wasn't over yet. That realization sent an arctic breeze blowing through my soul, so I burrowed into Mason's embrace, allowing his heat to beat back the persistent chill. "Was your dad mad that I couldn't answer his question about my past?" He certainly didn't seem pleased. After I told him I had no idea what Aunt Millie had been talking about, he got up and left the room.

"Not at you. He's a warlock, remember?"

How could I forget? Warlocks usually responded with anger when faced with situations beyond their control. It was their go-to emotion, which often annoyed me. Mason obviously sensed my frustration. He rubbed my back the way he sometimes did when I had trouble falling asleep. Each stroke somehow managed to rip the fears and stress from my body. His touch was all the magic I needed. "He just left to contact the other protector covens and fill them in on what happened."

Maybe one of them would have an answer. After all, the Proctor witches and the Stonewall wizards worked alongside the Blackmoors to protect the Gate, the source of all magic, from outside threats. Besides their bosses in the Conclave, the Proctors, Stonewalls, and Blackmoors were some of the most powerful members of the magical community. We'd defeated Ben and Sersie together. Hopefully we could do the same with Icarian and make him pay for what happened to Aunt Millie.

The slamming front door caught our attention. Pierce, Thad, and Aiden quickly rose, and Mason spun around, a black aura thrumming around his clenched fists. He'd activated his shadow powers and was ready to fight.

"Pierce!" cried a familiar voice from the foyer.

A smile spread across Pierce's features, but when he registered the distressed tone, he sprinted out of the living room and down the long hallway. "Kale?"

We stampeded after him, and by the time we entered the foyer, Pierce was holding him in a strong embrace. Kale served as the chief advisor for Caspian, the new Beast King. But even more importantly, Kale was the newest member of our ever-growing family. He still spent most of his time on Aeaea, which was why he was wearing the white tunic of his station, helping to rebuild the island after what Ben and Sersie did to it. Whenever Kale came to visit, his arrival made everyone happy, not just because he was a good guy but because the normally ornery Pierce turned sweeter than stolen honey.

But judging from Kale's panicked golden eyes, the event was more bitter than sweet. Was what Aunt Millie warned me about already here?

Pierce ran his hands over Kale's face as he gave him the once-over, obviously searching for any sign of injury. "Are you okay?"

"I'm better." The light of his smile reflected in his golden eyes as he pressed his lips to Pierce's, and Kale's tense body immediately relaxed. Whatever crisis had caused him to come flying all the way from his home had been forgotten in the arms and kisses of the man he loved.

When Pierce ran his hands down to Kale's butt and squeezed, Thad cleared his throat to remind them they were not alone. Pierce grumbled at the interruption, but when Kale glanced over Pierce's shoulder at us, his flushed cheeks blanched and his golden gaze grew dark. Something was definitely wrong.

"What's happened?" Thad asked.

Kale untangled himself from Pierce's arms and bit his lip. Whatever it was, he probably didn't want to speak the words. He only ever did that when he was nervous and afraid. "King Caspian's crown is gone."

The words hit me like a punch to the gut. After everything we'd done on Aeaea to keep Ben from stealing the crown of the Beast King, how could it possibly be gone now? But more importantly, why did I have a sneaking suspicion this had something to do with Aunt Millie's cryptic message?

SHORTLY AFTER Kale dropped his bomb on us, we made our way to the library as if we were on autopilot. It was where we gathered during times of distress and where we came up with plans on how to deal with the latest problems magic had presented us with. Over the past few months, we'd spent far too much time in that room.

Thad sat at his usual place on the piano bench. His hands were clasped, his index fingers pointing up and pressed to his lips. He was in what Pierce called his brainiac pose, no doubt searching for solutions. As always, Aiden stood at his side, but the gentle fairy had disappeared. Whenever danger called, Aiden turned into a bundle of tense muscle waiting to rip to shreds any threat that got close to Thad. Pierce and Mason weren't exactly happy campers either. Fury rolled across their expressions as they paced around the room. All our hard work the month before had been for nothing. I half expected their blue eyes to suddenly turn into burning coals.

Kale was the only one who hadn't been swallowed up by strategy or rage, which was probably due to his usually timid, dovelike nature. He tilted his head to one side and regarded me carefully, as if his avian eyes could see straight into my soul. "How have you been?" he asked before pulling me into a big hug.

What the heck had Kale been eating? The force of his embrace almost cracked a rib, and he was smaller than I was. Apparently the growth of his shifting ability had an effect on more than just the form he took when he shifted. It also made him a lot stronger than I remembered.

"I'll be better once you stop squeezin' the stuffin' out of me."

He immediately let me go. His golden eyes were hooded in concern. "Are you okay? Did I hurt you?"

When the breath returned to my lungs, I answered, "I'm better now."

"I'm sorry. I forget how strong I am these days."

No duh. I was going to be sore until next week. "Don't worry about it. I'll live."

"Can we focus, please?" Pierce moved behind Kale. Although his voice was stern, anger no longer turned his gaze into a stormy, blue sky. Looking at Kale had blown away the thunderclouds. "We've got a big pile of shit to deal with."

Kale exhaled. "I know."

Pierce shifted his gaze from him to me and back again. "You only know half of it."

"What do you mean?"

After Pierce caught Kale up about the events involving Aunt Millie, Kale once again swallowed me up in an embrace. "I'm so sorry, Drake."

"Thank you" was all I could manage in Kale's iron grip.

He immediately released me and flashed me a thin smile, apologizing for almost suffocating me again. I gripped Kale's hands and squeezed them. Even though he now shifted into an eagle, he'd always be a dove first. "Your turn. What happened?"

"Are you certain?" He glanced nervously around the room. "You have enough to deal with right now."

I appreciated his concern, but Kale was forgetting something. "You're family now too. Your problems are our problems."

Pierce grinned at me in appreciation before rubbing his hand up and down Kale's back. "Tell us what happened to the crown."

Kale blew all the air out of his lungs. "We aren't certain. King Caspian kept the crown on his person after what Ben did to King Alexander in order to procure it." Kale's gaze fell to the floor. He had served as King Alexander's personal emissary and had loved his former ruler very much. "But this morning he discovered it had been taken from him while he slept, and a thorough search of the island revealed it was no longer on Aeaea."

Only the Beast King and the Conclave possessed the power to breach the spell that kept Aeaea separate from our world. If this was Icarian's handiwork, then the power he wielded was even greater than we imagined. Not only had Icarian broken through a powerful enchantment and sneaked into Aeaea, something that hadn't been possible a few weeks ago, but he also managed to do it without being detected. "This means Icarian is stronger than we thought earlier, right?"

Thad, who usually held all the answers we needed, closed his eyes and frowned. "That's a logical assumption, yes."

"But how? Icarian needed Ben and Sersie to weasel their way onto Aeaea durin' Yule in order to steal the Air Crest that was on the crown."

"It has to be the crests." Pierce took his usual spot behind Kale and wrapped his arm around his boyfriend. Just like Aiden, he had his guard up. Pierce glanced around the room, waiting for an attack from the shadows. "They're talismans, right? That means they're linked to the magical elements that power us and get their energy directly from the Gate. Since the Gate is the source of all magic, Icarian must be using the talismans to boost his power."

Aiden shuddered. "So when he has all five he'll be unstoppable?"

"That would be my guess," Thad replied as he took Aiden's hand.

The world spun around me. What good would I be against this type of threat? Sure, I had immunity to most magic, but I wasn't magical. I was human. "This isn't good."

"No, Drake, it isn't." Mr. Blackmoor entered the library and crossed over to Kale. After giving his newest son his customary papa bear hug, he ran his hands through his dark hair and let out a frustrated sigh. "This isn't good at all. In fact, things only seem to be getting worse."

Thad closed the Grimoire and grumbled. "If Icarian has the Air Crest, the Fire Crest, and the Earth Crest, this means he may now have power that equals the Conclave's."

That was a sobering concept. The Conclave possessed abilities that surpassed everyone else's. Not only were they capable of casting spells to take down anyone in this room without breaking a sweat, they accessed their magic with only their thoughts. They didn't need to recite spells like Mason and his brothers or even gesture like Mr. Blackmoor. That meant Icarian could not only go toe-to-toe with nine of the most powerful witches, wizards, and warlocks, but he could eliminate any one of us with a stray thought.

"And Icarian only needs two more crests before the Spell Fall," I muttered.

Thad rose, placed his hands behind his back, and paced around the room. He did that when he had a solution or was completely frustrated. "No matter how many books I've read, I've yet to come across any mention of this Spell Fall Gerald Wa mentioned on Aeaea."

The Blackmoors and the other protector covens had been worrying themselves sick over the Spell Fall since Gerald's cryptic warning. He might still blame the Blackmoors and their secrets for bringing the magical community to this dangerous time, but the Conclave and *their* secrets were really to blame. "We need to contact the Conclave. We need to make them tell us about the Spell Fall and fill them in on what happened on Aeaea and with Aunt Millie."

Thad frowned. "But they haven't spoken to us for weeks."

Mr. Blackmoor had been a mass of anxiety ever since the Conclave threatened to replace the Blackmoors with the Edwells as the protector coven for the warlocks' magical caste, the Order of the Black. But tonight a fire once again roared in his eyes, and I was glad to see it. He reminded me of the warlock I first met, the one filled with confidence and purpose.

"Then there's only one thing left to do." A devious smile hitched up the corners of his lips. "We need to get their attention."

Mason mimicked his father's mischievous grin. He liked the way this was going. "When?"

"Tomorrow night at the Sabbat."

Thad surveyed the room with one eyebrow arched before returning his attention to his father. "But how are you planning to do this?"

He laced his fingers together and nodded toward the hallway. "Head upstairs and get some rest. It'll all be taken care of tomorrow."

CHAPTER 3

SWIRLING FINGERS of fog wrapped around me, blocking my view of the dilapidated house. The looming structure called to me, as if I'd been here before or at the very least seen a picture of it, but I couldn't recall when or where.

While the building looked familiar, the landscape did not. A bone-white mountain jutted into the sky behind the house. Tendrils of mist snatched at the mountain's heels as the fog slowly curled its way up the wrinkled face, trailing its long, white cloak down the slope and into the valley where the house and I both stood.

A sudden breeze sent chills down my spine and parted the veil, revealing a broken concrete walkway leading up to a wraparound porch. Weeds and dandelions sprouted from the cracks. An overgrown lawn had intruded into what used to be a garden, where the huge, red blooms of the rosebushes fought a fruitless battle against the green invaders.

Vines from the garden twisted up the exterior walls, which were covered in black blotches from years of neglect. Judging from the flecks of blue paint that still clung to the wooden slats, the house had once been vibrant and welcoming instead of a place where evil resided.

My breath hitched. What evil?

I had no clue why the thought entered my mind, but my heart raced in response. My brain screamed at me to get out of there, but my feet moved forward with purpose, as if they were ignorant to the fear that paralyzed me on the inside.

Even though I tried to stop, I continued down the path and up the creaking steps. What the hell was going on with my feet? A quick downward glance revealed a pair of tan-and-cream two-tone shoes I didn't own and that were certainly not in style. Even stranger were the objects I held in both hands, which I couldn't see clearly. My vision turned blurry, as if my mind had trouble interpreting what it saw.

The item in my right hand had to be a gun, based on the feel and weight of the cool metal grip. Whatever I held in my left hand, though, didn't make sense to my fingers. Its handle was thin and slick and ended in a bizarre dome that rested against the top of my closed fist.

"It must be done."

The words came out of my mouth without me realizing I had spoken them, and they sounded strange. It was almost as if it wasn't me, though my ears and the rumble of the words in my chest told a different story.

What was going on?

I stood before the entrance, steeling myself for whatever awaited me. With one strong kick, I struck the door, which exploded inward. Before I could enter, an alarm pierced through the void, dragging me backward and farther from the house and finally depositing me onto the bed I shared with Mason.

"Will you turn off the damned thing already?"

My eyes fluttered open to the morning light streaming through the bedroom curtains. Mason pulled the covers over his head and grumbled as my alarm continued to warn of an impending nuclear meltdown.

I switched off the clock on the nightstand, thrilled to be able to see my hands again. That had to be the most bizarre dream of my life, but considering what I'd been through with Aunt Millie, it wasn't all that surprising. It was most likely my subconscious trying to cope with the pain and guilt. Kale's news probably didn't help either.

We had a lot to face tonight when we gathered to celebrate Imbolc. The Sabbat marked the halfway point between the Winter Solstice and the Spring Equinox. It was to be a festival of light, so why did it feel like only darkness ever surrounded us?

Mason's low snore pulled me from my thoughts, which was a good thing. I couldn't dwell in the negativity anymore. No matter how hard it was, I had to do what my papa always said and point my shoes in the direction I wanted to go. Right now that direction was school, which Mason was never in a rush to get to. I slid off the mattress, grabbed the sheets, and yanked them free of the bed.

Mason yelped in surprise, curling into a naked ball. "What the hell? It's cold!"

He was right. It was cold, but for me, the chill was more internal than external. "We need to get to class."

Mason groaned and covered his face with a pillow. "Why can't we take the day off?" His words were strangled, but after a few months of trying to coax Mason out of bed, I'd grown fluent in his muffled-pillow voice. "We could use a mental health day after yesterday."

That was the God's honest truth, but staying home meant I'd obsess over Aunt Millie, the stolen crest, and the Spell Fall. Distracting myself with the routine of school would keep me sane. "Because we both have a big test comin' up over *King Lear*."

Mason threw the pillow across the room. "Stupid Shakespeare. Why can't he just write like a regular person?"

I loved Mason dearly, but his idea of a "regular person" was Dr. Seuss. "I'm gonna hop in the shower. You get ready."

Mason perked up. "Shower?"

I pointed at him as I approached the bathroom door. "You. *Stay*."

"Drake, wait."

I paused at the doorway and glanced back. "What?"

"It's probably a stupid question. Well, it is a stupid question, but how are… I mean after what happened…." He cursed and took a deep breath. "I just want to know if you're doing okay."

I wasn't, but I'd get there eventually. I just had to keep focused on the fact that I did what Aunt Millie wanted. If she were here, she'd be shooing me into the bathroom, fussing at me to not let what happened to an old woman stop me from living my life. "I'm hangin' in there."

"Is there anything I can do?"

I blew him a kiss. "Just be you."

"In that case." He got out of bed. "It's shower time."

I rolled my eyes and shut the bathroom door behind me and locked it. It wouldn't keep Mason out if he wanted to get in. That magic of his was a real pain in the ass sometimes. But hopefully the click of the lock would drive home my point.

I opened the glass shower door, set the temperature to a hair below scalding, and stepped into the spray.

The sting of the hot water pounded the tense bundle of muscles in my shoulders as my mind drifted back to the weird house in my dream. I still couldn't get over how strangely familiar that house was. It made the back of my brain itch something fierce. If I could just scratch it, I might find an answer.

Not that understanding a dream was important in the grand scheme of things. We had enough mysteries to solve. I forced the dilapidated house in the mist-shrouded valley out of my mind and dunked my head under the stream, losing myself in the comforting white noise of the water raining down around me.

"Need a hand?" The seductive purr of Mason's voice startled me.

Why did I have to tell Mason to continue being himself? I should have told him to be anyone *but* himself. I turned around, prepared to scold him for not listening to me and for potentially making me late, but his naked, tanned flesh coated in mist from the shower spray wrestled the words from my lips.

It was hard to be angry or to feel sad when Mason's electric gaze settled upon me. Of course being naked and dripping wet didn't hurt either. Maybe I was right all along. Maybe Mason being Mason was just what I needed.

Still, I wasn't letting him off the hook that easily. "Just a hand?" I pulled him into my arms and the hot deluge.

"It's hot. It's hot. It's hot." He jumped backward, wiping the searing water from his skin. His blue eyes lost their seductive twinkle, and his swelling hardness quickly deflated. "How the hell does your skin not melt off?"

I snickered and lowered the water temperature a few degrees for my sensitive-skinned boyfriend. Mason preferred showers that were usually too cold for my taste. Showers were meant to relax you, not cause shivering. "It's better than freezin' your ass off."

Mason rolled his eyes and grabbed the bodywash. Whenever we showered together, we argued about the water temperature. It had become part of our routine, and it comforted more than an embrace. "Yeah, well, I'm not a fan of ashy skin." He poured the liquid soap into his palm. "And whenever I shower with you, I itch all damn day."

"And when I shower with you, I get frostbite."

"Exaggerate much?" He motioned for me to turn around.

I did as instructed and stepped back under the water, which was verging on being chilly, while he spread his soapy hands up and down my back. "It's not exaggeratin' when my teeth are chatterin'."

"You're such a drama queen," he said with a playful smack to my ass.

I glowered at him over my shoulder. He waggled his bushy eyebrows as he rhythmically massaged the soap onto my skin in long, slow, circular motions. Damn, he was good. I had to close my eyes and think about dead kittens to keep from falling under his spell. "This from the warlock who fusses about everythin' under the sun?"

"I don't fuss." He ran his hands down my back before kissing my shoulder.

"Oh my God. Why do you have to fib so much?"

Mason stared down his nose at me. "Who's fibbin'?" he asked, imitating my Southern drawl.

"What were you sayin' about Imbolc last night?"

Mason cursed and launched into his rant about commemorating the Sabbat with the other protector covens. He had complained at least a hundred times in the past week. The Proctors were lame and the Stonewalls were stuck-up pricks. He'd said pretty much the same thing before the two other Wiccan holidays I'd observed with Mason, his family, and the rest of the magical community.

Like with most celebrations with friends and family, there was drama, but the Blackmoors amped it up a few notches. While many gatherings in the human community had to deal with drunken uncles or spats between siblings, each magical holiday I attended concluded with banshees attacking, shifters searching for help, or a whole buttload of trouble.

Based on the devious glint in Mr. Blackmoor's eyes last night, Imbolc would likely be no different.

"I swear if Miranda goads me again at this ritual, I'm gonna hex her stupid face." Mason punctuated the statement with one firm nod.

I rolled my eyes. I liked Miranda Proctor, but to Mason she was the devil incarnate. "That sounds like a lot of fussin' for someone who claims not to fuss."

"Oh really?" Mason pressed his naked, wet body against mine and slid his hand into my crevice, his finger around my hole. My breath hitched. I couldn't be late, but I couldn't concentrate on anything but Mason's finger prodding my opening or his hot breath pluming across my neck. Darn him and his magical fingers. "Do you hear any fussing now?"

All I could hear was the blood rushing toward my throbbing erection. God, I had to stop this. I had to be stronger than Mason's soapy hand around my cock, gently tugging my hardness while its mate continued to dance around the muscled rim of my ass.

"How about now?"

A low moan escaped my throat when Mason slipped his finger inside. How could I answer him when I could barely breathe? "I c-can't... be... late."

"Drake?" His warm breath pulsed across my neck.

"Yeah."

He pressed his lips to my flesh, nibbling a path up to my earlobe, leaving me breathless. "I really need you right now. I need to know everything is going to be okay. That *we* are going to be okay."

Oh God. I needed that too. Uncertainty stretched before us like a country road at midnight, and Mason's touch powered the headlights in the car we traveled together. He reminded me I was safe, loved, and protected, and right now, we both had to cling as tightly to those emotions as possible.

I turned around in his arms, pressing my soap-slick body against his. "I need that from you too."

Mason rested his hands on my hips and pressed a kiss to my nose. "Are you sure? I don't want you to get mad at me for making you late to school."

Being tardy a few minutes didn't matter as much as my need to embrace the love that grew hard between us. Instead of answering Mason's question, I wrapped my arms around his neck, surfed my fingertips down the curve of his back, and mounted my lips upon his.

Mason groaned into the kiss, his passion for life and for me grinding against my upper thigh. It had been too long since we last made love. Some new threat always seemed to get in our way, but nothing could stop us now. He was as eager to taste my flesh as I was to devour his. He worked his hands to my lower back, where he teased the swell of my backside.

I shuddered and slipped my tongue farther into his mouth, drinking him deep as he slid his fingers up and down my crevice. Mason's true power didn't come from his spells. It lived in the soothing of his fingertips.

"I've missed being with you," he panted, pushing his wet body against mine and trapping me against the cold tile.

"God, me too," I moaned as he danced his finger around my entrance. He shoved his cock against my soap-slick skin, and with each thrust against me, Mason reminded me of the power of our connection.

He grabbed my wrists and restrained them over my head. A devilish twinkle lit up his face, and I bit my lip. I knew what was next. He nibbled on my neck, biting a fiery trail down to my nipples. He wrapped his tongue around one, teasing the swelling nub with long licks and playful nips. My body shook, and low moans of pleasure escaped my throat.

By the time he took my other nipple in his mouth, my legs had turned wobbly and I felt light-headed. My cock throbbed with want as he wrapped a soapy hand around it, gently tugging my hardness while continuing to dance his fingers around the muscled rim of my ass.

"I love you so much," he muttered before slipping a finger inside me. My breath hitched as he drew circles within my body. His flesh against mine, his tongue on my nipples, his finger in my ass reminded me that whatever awful event came next didn't have the power to come between what lived inside the two of us.

"I love you too." My voice came out low and breathy as Mason jacked my cock harder and faster. I pushed into his grip, giving myself over to more than the rhythmic pulses his fingers sent rippling through me.

I surrendered myself and all my fears to the boy I loved, the one I knew would always be by my side.

Mason hummed, kissing my ear and my neck as he continued to cast his magic upon my sizzling flesh. "I think it's time. What do you think?"

"Darn straight." I lowered my hands, running them across his shoulders and down to his waist as I pressed my lips to his. His tongue immediately found mine and drew me into his mouth. As our tongues danced, I clutched his chest. I massaged his pecs and took his nipples between my thumbs and forefingers, causing them to stiffen and grow sensitive.

Low moans escaped Mason's throat, and his body trembled. He ran his hands down my stomach, charting a burning path to my throbbing cock, which longed for his touch. When he took me in his palm again, I gasped and molded my lips to his.

I skimmed my hands down his smooth sides and around to his firm ass. I grabbed a handful and pressed his body against my throbbing cock before pulling out of the kiss. "Except this time, it's my turn."

Mason leered at me, a sly grin cutting a path across his features. Over the past few months of our relationship, I had topped Mason only a handful of times. He preferred being the dominant one, most likely because his warlock nature demanded to be in control at all times. I certainly never complained. When Mason made love to me, when my body wrapped completely around his, I about crawled out of my skin.

Every time Mason penetrated my body, his love for me pressed deeper into my soul. Even though I still longed to experience that toe-curling, soul-shattering moment, what my heart and my soul craved was not to have Mason's love inside me but to plant mine deep within him.

I spun him around and nudged him forward. He braced himself against the tiled wall and arched his back, giving me the access I needed.

I dropped to my knees. As the warm water fell around me, I parted Mason's firm cheeks and licked lazy circles around his opening, which smelled like a heady mixture of morning musk and soap. Mason moaned and shuddered as I danced my tongue along the rim and across the puckered flesh, teasing the center with quick flicks before once again tracing a path along the outer rim.

"Man, Drake," he panted. "That feels awesome."

I growled in reply before pushing inside. Mason gasped as I probed and fluttered my tongue within him. He bucked, pressing his ass harder against my mouth, his trembling body begging for more.

And I was going to give it to him because this was something we both needed. This moment in time was going to carry us through the darkness.

I stood up and leaned over Mason. I pressed my chest to his back and inhaled the scent of desire and sweat that slowly replaced the spicy cinnamon of the bath soap. I licked a trail up his spine to the nape of his neck, where I delivered gentle kisses while nudging the length of my hardness against his crevice.

"Oh God yes." Mason turned his face to the side and devoured my lips as he ground his butt against my cock.

I pushed off Mason and grabbed my dick, pointing it toward his center. Mason watched me from over his shoulder. He wiped the snaking trails of sweat and shower spray from his flushed cheeks. Passion blazed in his blue eyes as he chewed his lower lip in anticipation.

As I locked gazes with Mason, I nudged the head of my cock against his hole. He held his breath, his eyes wide and eager as I slowly slipped inside the place that was truly my home.

"Yes," he panted, repeating the word over and over again as I slowly worked myself in and out of his butt. "That feels fucking awesome. We need to do this more often."

Yes, we did. We both needed to remember we were linked together forever, no matter what the future might bring, and in this crazy world of countless enemies trying to kill us, we had no clue what to expect once the sun rose on a new day.

I grabbed his shoulder with one hand and his waist with the other. With the leverage, I picked up speed, guiding Mason's body harder and faster against me.

"Oh yeah," Mason grunted. He clenched his teeth, slamming himself backward on my dick with the same force I drove into him. "This is what I needed. I love being with you like this, but not as much as I love you."

My body reacted to those words like they were a spell. Every muscle tensed as my impending climax churned. I leaned forward against Mason, my chest on his back as my hips took on a mind of their own. "I'm not gonna last much longer."

"Me either." Mason palmed his cock, matching the rhythm of our colliding bodies. He turned his face to the side again, pressing his lips to mine before his body shook in orgasm. Mason threw back his head and grunted as he shot four volleys of spunk onto the shower floor.

The spasming of his muscles and the soft moans of his release sent me over the edge. I shoved myself inside him one final time before my cock pulsed, filling Mason full of the love I produced only for him.

When I slid free, I pulled him to me and held him tight. "Have I told you that I love you?"

He turned around in my embrace and pressed his lips to mine. "You have, but I never get tired of hearing it, because I love you too."

My heart swelled. I might not know what was coming or where we were going, but Mason's love was like a compass.

It would always guide me home.

THANKS TO Mason's reckless driving, we made it to Havenbridge High in record time, and thanks to our mutually beneficial shower, the cold pricklies I'd woken up with didn't sting as sharply. The monotony of school routine also stabilized the churning chaos that swept me up in its never-ending waves, and I rode that crest all the way through my morning classes.

It wasn't until lunch that I realized something was up.

The moment I entered the cafeteria, the roar of conversation thundered even louder than usual, which was saying a lot for a group of kids who had zero concept of an inside voice. They normally sat in their assigned packs, screeching at each other across the table, but today they flitted around the room as if they couldn't contain themselves.

Since I'd moved here from Texas, I'd come to know there was only one thing that could rile them up like this: gossip. Judging by the animated gestures and constantly shuffling bodies, it was pretty juicy too.

"Drake!" Mason stood on the table, waving me over as if I had no clue where we'd been sitting for the past few months. A big grin plastered across his face and a twinkle lit up his eyes. He still had that after-sex glow, and I found it kind of hot.

I cut through the cafeteria to the table where he sat with Brandon Priestly, Simon Busby, and Eddie Harmon, his juvenile delinquent friends.

A large group of Chatty Cathys created a human barricade down the middle aisle. As I detoured around them, one of the girls squealed to her friends. "Have you *seen* him yet? He's so bae-worthy!" Her friends launched into high-pitched answers that told me all I needed to know. A new student had transferred into HHS, and the sharks smelled fresh blood.

After my detour and a few more zigs and a couple of zags, I finally made it to the table, where Mason gave me a kiss before stifling a yawn. He'd likely just woken from the nap he usually took in fourth period. "So has anyone seen the new kid?"

Mason's scowl was all the answer I needed.

"So I take it you have."

"I don't know what everyone's going on about." Mason took a big bite of his burger, continuing the conversation as he chewed. "He's nothing special."

Neither was watching Mason's food tumbling around in his mouth. I'd raised pigs with better table manners.

"Mase is right." The fact Brandon agreed with Mason wasn't a surprise. He agreed with anything Mason said. While he might terrorize most everyone else in school with his mass, he turned into a lapdog around Mason. "He couldn't be less specialer if he tried."

I'd given up trying to correct Brandon's grammar. It was a losing battle. "What did he do? Try to sit next to you in class?"

My answer earned me four sets of rolling eyes. On my first day at Havenbridge High, I had dared to sit with them at this very table, and I hadn't exactly been met with open arms. Each of them had tried to intimidate me, but they quickly learned I wasn't so easily scared off.

"No, but you should've been there when—"

A loud thwack echoed from under the table as Brandon's face contorted in pain. Had Mason just kicked him?

"When what?"

Brandon glanced down at the table while Simon and Eddie suddenly stuffed food into their mouths.

I panned to Mason. "What happened?"

"It was no big deal," he answered with a half grin. "Just had to let the new kid know I wasn't to be messed with."

That sounded all too familiar. "You mean like you tried to do to me on my first day?"

Mason rubbed his thumb down the nape of my neck, smiling at me as if that was the silliest question in the world. "Nope. Not like you at all. This was different, believe me."

"Definitely different." A big grin spread across Brandon's meaty face. "Besides, you're cool, and I like you now." If I was being completely honest, I'd grown to like him too. He reminded me of George from *Of Mice and Men*.

Simon and Eddie were tougher pills to swallow. Eddie emitted various gaseous explosions seemingly at will, while Simon was often crass, saying the first inappropriate thing that came to mind.

Simon leaned back on the bench, exposing the lettering on his T-shirt, which read *You're too chubby to be no fun*, and said, "Plus, the guy's a total douche."

Oh, the irony. "And you're an expert at identifyin' douches, huh?"

He sat up with his chin high while clicking his tongue. "Naturally."

Eddie let out a loud belch in agreement.

These two didn't spend much time looking in the mirror.

"I've got a question." Mason draped his arm around my shoulder and leaned in close, brushing his lips against my cheek. "Why are we still talking about him?"

I shrugged. "Just curious. The entire school seems to be chatterin' about him."

"Yeah, well, what we should be celebrating is another day of school without Miranda."

Brandon, Simon, and Eddie cheered like hooligans. Miranda wasn't exactly their favorite person. She had no qualms about cutting them off at the knees with her scalpel-sharp wit. "She must be really sick. Maybe I should give her a call."

Mason flinched as if I'd lit myself on fire. "Why on earth would you do that?"

I pulled my phone out of my pocket and scrolled through my contact list. "Because she's a friend." A round of snorts disagreed. "Well, she's *my* friend, and I'm worried about h—"

"Excuse me? Are you Drake Carpenter?"

I turned in my seat and gazed up into a pair of cornflower blue eyes. I'd never met anyone who had my eye color, and since I'd never seen this guy before, he had to be the new kid the school couldn't stop buzzing about. I could certainly see why. He had fair skin, smooth features, and a striking smile. His all-American look certainly explained what all the fuss had been about.

"If that's a no, you can just tell me to fuck off." He shook away the strands of sandy-blond hair that curled out of his knitted beanie and fell in front of his eyes.

Oh Lord. How long had I been staring? "I'm sorry. No."

"No worries. Must have the wrong guy." He turned on his heels and started to walk away.

Wait. What? "No. I mean, yes."

He glanced over his shoulder at me. A grin teased across his thin, pink lips. "Which is it, man? Yes or no?"

My cheeks grew hot. "Yes, I'm Drake, and no, I'm not tellin' you to fuck off."

"Yeah, well, maybe I am." Mason stood. Brandon, Simon, and Eddie immediately fell in behind him.

"Sweet!" The guy with the killer smile ignored Mason and held out his hand to me. "I'm Will Hopkins." I applauded his bravery, and I could see why he and Mason might have issues. Will was likely used to being at the top of the school's food chain, just like Mason.

I took his hand and returned his smile. "Nice to meet you, Will. Is there somethin' I can help you with?"

"Damn straight." Will slid into the seat next to me, and the move brought a gasp from the peanut gallery gathered behind me. It was hard to keep a straight face.

"What is it?"

"Principal Skinner said I should find you, that since you were the last kid to transfer here you might be okay with showing me the ropes."

"What?" Mason leaned over my shoulder. "Why does it have to be you?"

I cupped his cheek. "Do you want to do it?"

He scrunched up his lips and sat back down.

"Will, this is—"

"We've met," Mason and Will answered in unison. From the abruptness of their voices, it hadn't been a good first impression for either of them.

"Thanks for letting me join you." Will pulled a brown paper bag out of his backpack. "Lunch on the first day at a new school isn't exactly the highlight of the day."

That was no lie. "So when did you get into town?"

"Couple of days ago. So," Will said, nodding over at Mason, "I take it the two of you are boyfriends?"

Mason draped his arm over my shoulder. "Why? Do you have a problem with that?"

Brandon, Eddie, and Simon leaned closer, awaiting his answer.

"Nah," he said, waving off Mason's words. "I'm not a homophobic dick."

Mason grunted. "Well, at least you're not homophobic."

Will put down his sandwich and let out a big sigh. He sat sideways in his seat and looked over my shoulder at Mason. "Look, man. I know we didn't get off to a good start, but is there any way we can get past that?"

Mason didn't answer. He locked gazes with Will as if he were waiting for a rattlesnake to strike.

"Someone better tell me what the heck happened between you two."

Will bit his bottom lip. "I might have called your boyfriend stupid."

"No." Mason tapped his index finger once on the tabletop. "What you said was I was depriving a village somewhere of its idiot."

Mason's brothers called him an idiot all the time, and it irritated him to no end. He begrudgingly took it from them, but he never let anyone else get away with calling him names. It was one of the reasons he walked around with such a big chip on his shoulder at school, to prevent anyone else from trying to tease him.

I held Mason's hand tightly in mine in a show of solidarity. "Yeah, that wasn't very nice."

Will nodded. "I know, but I wouldn't have done it if Mason hadn't been scowling at me from the moment I walked into the classroom. I've faced enough bullshit at all my other schools."

His explanation made perfect sense to me. "Is that true? Were you scowlin' at him?"

Mason scrunched up his lips and shrugged.

"Sure you were!" Brandon pointed out. "You always scowl at the new kids."

Mason cut his gaze to Brandon, who quickly shut up while Simon and Eddie hid their laughter behind their hands.

"So how about this?" I unclenched Mason's fist and straightened out his fingers. "Why don't the two of you shake hands, call a truce, and start over?"

Will held out his hand. "I'm game."

When Mason didn't respond, I nudged him with my knee.

"Fine." He took Will's hand and gave it a shake. "But I'm doing this for Drake, not for you."

A smile spread across Will's face. "Well, we've got to start somewhere, right?"

I couldn't agree more, but Mason obviously wasn't convinced. He tilted his head to one side as if he were mentally weighing evidence that no one else could see.

I HEADED straight for my locker after the final bell rang for the day. Mason and I were under strict orders from Mr. Blackmoor to come straight home. He wanted everyone dressed so we could head over to the Stonewalls' on time. Whatever he had planned to get the Conclave's attention evidently couldn't wait one minute longer than necessary.

The chaos that enveloped our lives had to stop. In order for that to happen, we needed answers only the Conclave could give.

I threw the books I didn't need over the weekend into my locker and tossed the ones I did into my backpack before heading out the front doors to wait in Mason's car for him, because he had detention again.

A cold breeze immediately stung my exposed skin as I left the warmth of the building. I zipped up my leather jacket, shoved my hands in my pockets, and darted down the front steps. I spotted Will shivering a few feet away.

"Hey!"

He looked up from his cell phone and smiled. "What's up, bro?"

"Just wonderin' why you're freezin' your butt off out here instead of stayin' inside where it's warm."

"Just waiting for my dad to come pick me up." He held up his phone and rolled his eyes. "He just texted that he's on his way."

Will glanced behind me before settling his gaze back on me. "Where's Mason?"

"Detention."

He nodded. "Sounds about right."

Well, that truce didn't last long. "I thought you two were gonna try and bury the hatchet."

Will shoved his phone back into his pocket and shifted his weight from one foot to the other in an obvious attempt to keep warm. "I'm willing, but I don't think your boyfriend is up for it."

He wasn't wrong. Even though Mason had agreed, he didn't do so willingly. "Just give him time. It takes Mason a while to warm up."

Heck, after I met Mason, it took a few weeks before I lost the urge to punch him in the face, and we were spell bound. Will and Mason might take a bit longer.

"If you say so." He shrugged. "I'm just surprised he let you out of his sight. He seems to never leave your side."

Although Will apparently meant the comment as a dig, I didn't take it that way. I loved the way Mason craved being next to me, found excuses to touch me. It made me feel special, as if there was no other place he'd rather be, and the feeling was definitely mutual.

Will chuckled. "You've been apart for more than fifteen minutes already. I'm surprised he hasn't sent out a search party yet."

I glanced at my watch before grinning up at him. "Not for another fifteen minutes or so."

Will snickered as a car pulled up next to us. The passenger's side window rolled down. An older, more rugged version of Will peered up at us from the driver's seat. The square cut of his jaw and his almost-bald head reminded me of a Marine. Even though he smiled up at us, the hardness of his features never softened. The only gentle part about him was the soft blue of his eyes.

"Hey, son. I see you made a new friend like I told you to."

Will clenched his jaw as he opened the car door. "Dad, this is Drake."

I stepped toward the car and extended my hand. "Nice to meet you, Mr. Hopkins."

His grip was strong and extremely firm. He shook hands as if he had something to prove. "Good to meet you, Drake. Please, call me Flint."

I'd never had one of my friends' parents ask to be called by their first name before. That was just not how things were done in the South. If you weren't saying "Yes, ma'am" or "Yes, sir," you could almost be guaranteed a scolding by your parents. "That may take some gettin' used to, sir, but I can try."

"A young man with manners." He glanced at Will and motioned to me. "They *do* exist."

"Whatever," Will huffed as he got into the car. "Let's go."

Mr. Hopkins shrugged at me and smiled as if the two of us were a part of a private joke. It was a little strange.

"Drake!" Mason bounded down the steps behind me and came sprinting to my side. "I'm free at last! Free at last!"

When he grabbed my hand and kissed my cheek, Mr. Hopkins's creepy smile beat a hasty retreat. "Well, we should be going."

I nodded. It seemed Mr. Hopkins was the homophobic prick in the family. "See you later, Will."

He gave me a silent nod before the car drove away.

CHAPTER 4

SHORTLY AFTER Mason and I got home, we changed into our clothes for the Sabbat. Then the family piled into three different cars and followed Mr. Blackmoor to an old Victorian-style house belonging to the Stonewalls.

Mason exited his car and scowled at the white 4Runner parked out front. The vehicle belonged to the Proctors. "With any luck, Miranda's home in bed with the flu."

Mr. Blackmoor ascended the porch steps. "In order for this to work, we need everyone."

No one had a clue how Mr. Blackmoor intended on getting the Conclave's attention. Normally when he needed to speak with them, he'd use whatever spell only he and the other High Priests could cast that would open up a communication link, but the Conclave hadn't been responding to Mr. Blackmoor's attempts to contact them for weeks.

Judging from his set jaw, he had planned something that would put an end to the silent treatment.

The front door swung open, and Mrs. Stonewall stood at the entryway. As a wizard, she typically betrayed no emotion on her fair features. Her kind approached life with detached, cold logic, which made them hard to read. Tonight, the slight curl of her upper lip communicated she was more than a little annoyed. "Oliver, we have all gathered early as you requested." She held open the door and eyed each of us as we filed into her house. "I certainly could have used the extra time to prepare for the Sabbat. Perhaps now you wouldn't mind explaining why."

"I will," he replied as we all shed our coats and placed them on the hooks by the front door. "There have been a few developments."

She let out a long-suffering sigh. "Why is it that your family always seems to find themselves in the middle of these developments?"

"Maybe it's because we're the only ones capable of dealing with them." A wicked grin slanted across Mason's lips. He got his jollies by attempting to rile up the wizards. Mrs. Stonewall's illusion-casting abilities made prodding her a dangerous hobby.

"That's enough." His father's stern voice quickly wiped the smirk from Mason's lips, but the dancing light in Mr. Blackmoor's blue eyes told me that Mason being difficult was part of his plan. To Mrs. Stonewall, he said, "Shall we begin?"

Her only response was to walk past us and lead us into the living room. She had never been friendly, but she'd always been cordial in the past. Apparently those days were over.

Mr. Blackmoor either didn't notice or didn't care. He immediately crossed to where Mr. Stonewall and Mr. Proctor stood chatting at the far end of the room. It wasn't unusual for the High Priests to talk among themselves before addressing the rest of us.

Mrs. Stonewall and Mrs. Proctor huddled together by the fireplace, which had been covered with candles in celebration of Imbolc. They glanced over their shoulders at us and gave us the evil eye. Neither woman liked the Blackmoors all that much, but they liked me least of all. They didn't trust me because I was human and immune to their magic. Mason tugged me into a corner, away from where his brothers talked with their boyfriends.

"You look like someone just peed in your punch. What's wrong?"

I nodded toward where Mrs. Stonewall and Mrs. Proctor stood seething. "I guess it just bothers me that they hate me so much. I've done everythin' I can to be nice and polite to them, but nothin' I do seems to work."

"So stop trying. They're not worth it." He turned and met their piercing gazes with a scowl. The two women rolled their eyes and resumed their private conversation. "See? All better."

I couldn't help but laugh. My knight in not-so-shining armor had ridden to my rescue again. "You're such a goof."

"I'm your goof," he said with a playful nip at my nose. "And don't you forget it."

Like I ever could. No matter how crazy he might sometimes make me, Mason belonged to me as much as I belonged to him. He was forever my goof.

"Will you two get a room?"

Mason's bushy eyebrows pinched together at the sound of Miranda's voice behind us. He swatted the air at her as if she were a fly. "Shoo!"

Before Miranda's snarky reply could even form, I gave her a big hug and a smile. "How are you feelin'?" It had been at least three days since she'd last been in school.

She arched one eyebrow at Mason, letting him know she wasn't done with him, before she settled her dark brown eyes on me. "I'm fine. We've just been busy."

Her answer puzzled me. It wasn't like Miranda to miss school, especially since I had transferred into Havenbridge High. Before me, she'd been practically guaranteed to graduate as valedictorian. Now she had to fight me for the title, and she'd been doing so tooth and nail. Our friendly competition kept us both on our toes academically, so if it wasn't an illness that caused her to miss class, then something else was going down, something so big that she was willing to lose some of her lead in our grade skirmish. "With what?"

"Family stuff," she said to my sneakers.

Now I knew something was wrong. Miranda didn't avert her eyes for anyone. Whether it ticked someone off or not, she answered all questions with complete confidence and a steady gaze.

"Miranda, why won't you look at me?"

She lifted her gaze to mine, attempting to school her expression, but tiny flecks of discomfort swam within the depths of her brown eyes. "What? I'm looking right at you."

"Yeah, but you also look like you were caught with your hand in the cookie jar."

"I have no idea what you're talking about."

Mason pointed at her and cackled. "You're lying."

She narrowed her eyes. "I am not."

"You're doing it again," Mason shrieked in delight. Even though he was right, he was enjoying this a bit too much. He evidently didn't see that this wasn't a joking matter. "I never thought I'd see the day when a goody-goody witch would actually lie."

She snorted. "And who made you the expert on lying?"

"Are you kidding me?" Mason gaped at me as if he couldn't believe his ears before returning his attention to Miranda. "I've been lying since I learned how to talk. 'No, Pierce, I don't know who broke your football trophy.' 'Don't get angry with me, Thad. I have no idea what happened to that paper you spent all night writing.' 'Gee, Dad, I wasn't the one who scratched up the Jag. It was probably Pierce.'" When he stopped, he motioned to her as if he'd just made his case and won.

Miranda crossed her arms over her chest. "Fine, so you're not to be trusted. I already knew that, but I'm sure your boyfriend is thrilled to hear that bit of news."

Mason slowly panned to me, a big grin spreading wide across his lips. "Of course, I never lie to the boy I love."

Yeah right. "So what happened to my physics lab report I was working on last week?"

Mason sputtered like an old car.

"Don't hurt yourself," Miranda replied with a grin.

"How about you answer my question?" I narrowed my eyes at Miranda, who suddenly joined Mason in his sputtering jalopy.

"What's going on over here?" Edith Stonewall and her twin, Elliot, joined us, no doubt attracted by the smoke from the pants of the two liars standing before me.

Mason grumbled and shot me a fat bottom lip. "Drake's being mean."

Edith regarded me with cool blue eyes before glancing at Mason. "I know Drake and I know you. Obviously he's reacting to something you did."

I chuckled while Mason grumbled. Sometimes the cold logic of a wizard worked in your favor. "Thank you, Edith."

She nodded. "So what's going on? Elliot said we needed to get over here quick."

When all eyes turned to Elliot, he flushed. He didn't like being the focus of attention. That was most likely because he was teased at school for being mute. While Elliot might not be able to speak like most people, he communicated using his telepathy. That told me Elliot had been reading our thoughts and rushed his sister over here either to help me or save Miranda. It was time to find out which. "Miranda was just about to tell us why she's been out of school for the past few days."

Edith and Elliot glanced sideways at each other. They'd come for Miranda, not me.

"So the two of you know." It wasn't a question, and my three friends realized I was onto them.

Mason's shrug communicated he hadn't clued in yet. Bless his heart. "So what? Who cares if Miranda had diarrhea or was skipping class? All that matters is I've enjoyed three blissful days of school without the Wicked Witch of the West."

I grabbed Mason's shoulder and turned him toward me before Miranda had time to fire off a snarky missile. "Mason, you don't get it. Somethin' has happened, and they know about it."

Again he shrugged.

"That means we don't."

He still couldn't solve the puzzle. "So? We've had stuff happen to us. They don't know about it yet. That's why we're here. To fill them in."

Mason talked a big game, but he couldn't see the deception in people he believed were his friends even when it was staring him right in the face.

I cupped his cheek with my palm, which earned me the smile I loved gazing into. "Yes, you're right. We *are* here to tell them what happened with Aunt Millie and on Aeaea."

Miranda gasped. "Wait a minute. What?"

"What happened on Aeaea?" Edith asked.

Your aunt Millie's back? I winced as Elliot spoke in my head. His telepathy had the annoying side effect of causing migraines. *Is everything okay?*

I ignored their questions. Right now I wasn't pleased with any of them. "But whatever they know—"

"They weren't going to tell us." Mason turned and glared at them before grabbing my hand and tugging me away. "We need to get to Dad."

I nodded, but before Mason and I could take two steps, Mr. Blackmoor and the other High Priests announced they were ready to begin.

AFTER SEVERAL failed attempts to get his father's attention and tell him what we feared, Mason stood with me at the back of the living room while Mr. Blackmoor asked Kale to fill everyone in on the latest in Aeaea.

When he was done, a lengthy silence gobbled up all the breathable air in the room. Judging by the tense postures, everyone realized how much worse the situation had gotten, but the many bouncing gazes also revealed a sense of discomfort, as if no one knew what to do.

"So what now?" Miranda's older brother, Adam, was the first to break the silence.

Mr. Blackmoor crossed to the center of the room, and all eyes fell on him. "I'm glad you asked, Adam. We need to do something, and we need to do it fast."

"And why's that?" Mr. Proctor's casual tone seemed to challenge Mr. Blackmoor's urgency. Mr. Blackmoor's clenched jaw revealed he didn't appreciate being dismissed. Like Mason and Miranda, the two men didn't play well together, and it was starting to tick me off, especially since Mr. Proctor's demeanor basically verified my worst fear.

"How about the fact that my aunt Millie paid me a visit yesterday?"

That got their attention. Raised voices immediately filled the room as dozens of questions exploded all at once until they merged into a thundering roar. I had to raise my hand to get them to quiet down.

"Was anyone hurt?" Charlotte asked once everyone stopped speaking.

Mason grumbled. "She knocked me unconscious."

"Considering she's a monster, you should count yourself lucky you survived." Mr. Stonewall's thoughtless comment made Aiden and me bristle.

"That shows you how much you know. Before you go off spoutin' awful remarks about my family, you should hear what this 'monster' had to tell me first."

So I told them what Aunt Millie revealed about Icarian and about the danger he posed, but before I could fill them in on what she hinted about my past, Mr. Blackmoor gave my shoulder a squeeze. That was his way of telling me not to reveal that bit of information just yet.

Maybe I'd been wrong. Perhaps Mr. Blackmoor did realize what was going on with the other protector covens.

"So as you can see," Mr. Blackmoor said once he realized his message had been received, "we need to act fast. Now that we know Icarian's name, we can work on constructing a spell that will find him. Then we can retrieve the crests he's already stolen and put an end to his threat once and for all. Luckily, I've come up with a plan. Some of us need to head back to Aeaea to see if we can find any residual magic we might be able to follow to Icarian. It makes sense for my family to travel back with Kale while the rest of you see if you can locate Icarian with a modified scrying spell."

While Thad discussed spells that might allow the Stonewalls and the Proctors to do just that, the members of the other two protector covens glanced at each other. Adam scratched his chin while Charlotte tilted her head to one side. Miranda fidgeted with her hands, dragging her gaze back and forth from her mother, who couldn't seem to tear her steady gaze off Thad, to everyone else in the room. As for the Stonewalls, they regarded Thad with the exact same expression: pinched eyebrows and narrowed eyes.

"So what do you think?" Thad asked, oblivious to the attitude change.

Mrs. Stonewall cleared her throat. "I think you've lost your mind."

Thad flinched, and though his lips moved, shock had stolen the breath from his lungs.

"What are you talking about?" Even though Mr. Blackmoor acted surprised, his arms crossed over his chest told the truth. He'd been expecting that answer. "We've come up with a good plan."

"Yes, well, you've also completely forgotten that we answer to the Conclave." Mrs. Proctor smoothed the creases in her long white skirt and sat back in her chair. "We make no move until we receive our orders."

"You've got to be fucking kidding me." Pierce stood up, the tendons in his neck fanned out in rage. "We've been handed information we can use to find the bad guy and you want to sit and wait for orders? You're the one who's lost her mind."

Adam suddenly stood between Pierce and his mother. Although the two of them had worked out their previous differences, it was clear that Adam wouldn't let Pierce get away with yelling at his mother. "Back down, Pierce." He took a step to decrease the distance between them. "Now."

"Oh, come on, Adam." Pierce gripped his best friend's shoulders in what appeared to be frustration and not anger. "You know better than anyone else that the Conclave wants nothing to do with us. They made that clear when they abandoned us in Aeaea."

"Pierce is right." Mason let go of my hand and joined his brother's side. "They haven't spoken to us since then. What makes you think they're gonna start now?"

"You've made a faulty leap in logic." Mr. Stonewall rose from his chair. Although his words were firm, no anger painted the tones of his voice. "The Conclave hasn't spoken to *you*."

Pierce and Thad gaped at Mr. Stonewall before turning their wide-eyed gazes to their father. Mr. Blackmoor let out a deep sigh. He'd apparently seen that coming. "What exactly does that mean, Lawrence?"

"It means just that," Mr. Stonewall answered. "Just because your family has not heard from the Conclave doesn't mean that mine or the Proctors have not."

Mr. Blackmoor shot his steely gaze over to Mrs. Proctor, who only nodded in reply. "So you've spoken to them?"

Mrs. Proctor inhaled sharply before releasing a deep breath. Her stony persona gave way to a softer, gentler woman with eyes filled with regret. "Yes."

"They've done more than that." I moved to stand with Mr. Blackmoor and shook my head in disapproval at the others. "Miranda's been out of school for the last few days, and if I'm guessin' right, her coven has not only spoken with the Conclave but has been involved in some mission for them."

Mr. Blackmoor's right eye twitched. *That* he hadn't seen coming. "I see."

"What my coven has or has not done is not your concern." Mrs. Proctor rose and took two trembling steps toward us. "We cannot make a move while the Conclave is deciding how best to deal with this crisis."

This didn't make a hill of beans worth of sense. The Conclave had practically wet themselves at the mention of the Spell Fall. Now that another crest had been taken, why wouldn't they act? "And you're fine with that?"

Mrs. Proctor avoided eye contact. She opened her mouth to speak, but before the words could tumble from her lips, she noticed her husband's stoic gaze and took a deep breath. "The Conclave knows best."

She was lying. That couldn't be more obvious. But she was terrified of speaking her mind against the Conclave, just like everyone else *except* the Blackmoors.

"I don't buy it for one second," I said, pointing my finger at them. "You're afraid of going against the Conclave."

Mrs. Stonewall sat upright in her chair, and Mrs. Proctor took two steps back.

"Now is not the time for impertinence." Mr. Stonewall took a protective stance next to his wife. "This isn't about you or the Blackmoors' irrational need to challenge authority. This is about what's best for our community."

I snorted. "Now who's bein' illogical? The only ones who seem to be thinkin' about *this* community is *my* family."

"Drake's right." Mason returned Mr. Stonewall's steely gaze as he took my hand and stood at my side. "The only thing we care about is stopping Icarian. All you're concerned with is being good little soldiers."

"I think that's enough." Mr. Proctor stood on the opposite side of his wife, whose resolve to fall in line appeared to be fading. Her eyes filled with the same ire that fanned in ours, but one glance at her husband and Rachel Stonewall quickly doused those flames.

"No, it's not." It was Pierce's turn to join in. He locked eyes with Adam and Edith. "The two of you were on Aeaea with us. You heard firsthand the secrets the Conclave had been keeping from us. They had been using the fae and the shifters for their own needs and didn't bother telling *any* of us about the Crests of the Five."

"Or explain what the Spell Fall is," Thad added.

"Their lies led to the destruction in Otherworld," Aiden said, taking his place next to Thad.

Kale nodded. "And to Aeaea being burned to the ground."

"They were trying to protect us." Charlotte's voice was barely a whisper. "Weren't they?" Her resolve continued to fall, just like her mother's, which was ironic. Mrs. Proctor and Charlotte had been two of the staunchest supporters of the Conclave.

"No, Charlotte," Mr. Blackmoor stated. "The Conclave was trying to protect themselves."

"Oliver, that's enough!" Mr. Stonewall railed.

"No, Lawrence. It is *not*!"

"And that is where you are wrong, Oliver Blackmoor. Once again."

Suddenly nine robed and hooded figures stood in the Stonewall living room: three in white, three in gray, and three in black. The Conclave had finally broken their silence.

CHAPTER 5

QUIET DESCENDED upon the room after the Conclave poofed into existence. It had been weeks since we last saw them, and we hadn't parted on the best of terms. Gerald Wa, our previous ally in the Conclave, withdrew support when he believed we'd turned our backs on him. The man might be one of the most powerful wizards on earth, but he couldn't tell his rear from a hole in the ground.

The Conclave were the ones who had turned their backs on us and treated everyone from the fae and shifters all the way to their supposedly heralded protector covens as chess pieces in some cosmic game. They didn't care about others. Power and secrecy seemed to be their driving motivation.

For the first time, the birth of witch hunters made absolute sense. If the Conclave were the types of magical beings humans first came across, no wonder they were hunted down. Power such as theirs didn't belong in this world, especially if its wielders were corrupt.

"We see the Blackmoors have yet to learn their lesson," said one of the hooded figures in black. The odd metallic tone to her voice marked her as the same warlock who had attacked Mason and Pierce during Yule—the one Pierce referred to as the Warlock Hag. Why she altered her voice never made any sense to me. What was she trying to hide? She glided forward as she spoke, revealing she was evidently the new voice of the Conclave. Gerald would no longer speak to us or on our behalf.

She and the rest of Conclave stood before us, their bodies rigid. Although I couldn't see their eyes from within their shadowed hoods, it didn't take a genius to know their gazes were boring to the depths of our souls.

They were searching for the truth, trying to learn if the Blackmoors had truly turned traitor. At least, that was the way they saw things. To them, any dissension was a punishable offense. Their word was law, and their will was to be obeyed.

"Have you nothing to say for yourself?" the Warlock Hag asked after a few moments of weighted silence.

Mr. Blackmoor held his chin high and clasped his hands behind his back. "I was uncertain if you were actually speaking to us now."

She tensed, and if she didn't get her temper under control, Mr. Blackmoor would find himself at the mercy of her terrible power. After a few breaths, her shoulders relaxed. "No. We see nothing has changed."

I stepped forward. "That's not true." What the hell was I doing? It wasn't my place to challenge their authority, especially since I'd witnessed firsthand what happened to those who did. Maybe it was my immunity to magic that made me feel invincible, but there was no way I was going to let that hag speak to Mr. Blackmoor like that. He was a good man with a big heart, and unlike the Conclave, his only motive was protecting others. "*Everythin'* has changed."

The Warlock Hag turned her hooded head to me. She was most likely shooting me daggers right now. "Our affairs are none of your concern, human."

"Is that your answer for everythin'? Am I human? Yeah. Big flippin' deal. It doesn't mean I don't care about the people in this room. Somethin' big is about to go down. You know it. We all know it, and I bet it will affect us all, magical *and* human."

Instead of replying to my outburst, the Warlock Hag floated over to me.

"Stay away from—" Invisible hands plucked Mason off his feet and dangled him in the air.

"Be a good boy and stay," she said. Mason writhed against the magic that kept him trapped, but no spell he cast or shadow form he weaved could ever set him free. She glanced at the rest of my family, who appeared to be two seconds away from rushing her. "I'd advise the rest of you to follow suit. Unlike Gerald, I will *not* be trifled with. Cross me at your own peril."

Although lightning streaked through Mr. Blackmoor's eyes, he placed his hands on his sons' shoulders and whispered to Kale and Aiden. Whatever words he spoke failed to have their desired effect on Aiden. His massive chest heaved like he was a wild mustang refusing to be tamed. Thankfully he didn't move. Even the hybrid abilities of a vampyre fae were nothing compared to the magic the Warlock Hag could access with a thought.

Once she was satisfied everyone would stay where she wanted them, she hovered before me. I didn't blink and I didn't back down. "You remain an anomaly, Drake Carpenter. One that has brought much discord to the Conclave."

Hearing that made me smile. I was glad to be a burr in their saddles.

"This brings you joy, I see."

Even though she hovered no more than six inches from my face, I still couldn't see anything but the black, endless void within her shadowed cowl. I locked on to where I thought her eyes would be and nodded. "Yes, it does."

She glided a few inches closer until my face was practically in her hood. "Why is that?"

"Because I'm probably the first person in more years than you can remember who you haven't been able to intimidate with magic."

"You think your immunity to our powers makes you better than us? Stronger, perhaps?"

"No. It makes me different. Just the way you were different when your species first evolved from humans. I'm no better than you, just as you are no better than me."

"Yet your attitude speaks otherwise." She floated back a few feet before turning to face the Blackmoors. "And so does that of your coven."

Confusion slowly replaced the searing anger that previously flushed Mr. Blackmoor's cheeks. "That has never been my intention." He took two tentative steps forward, obviously wanting to decrease the distance that had separated him from the Conclave over the past few months. Had this been his plan all along? "I merely wish to perform the duty my family has been appointed to. Protecting the Gate is my only motive, and whatever Icarian is planning places the Gate in jeopardy."

Her shoulders tensed. "You learned the true name of our foe? How?"

For a group of powerful magical beings, they sure didn't know a whole heck of a lot. "My aunt Millie."

She turned to face the rest of the Conclave. After a few moments, she faced forward. "This news surprises us." The rise in her pitch told me she was downright shocked. Had they not known this information before now? "But what brings you to the conclusion that the Gate is in danger?"

Kale stepped forward. "You mean besides the fact that King Caspian's crown has been stolen?"

"What?" She glanced over at the stiff bodies of the Conclave. "The Air Crest has been taken? When did this happen?"

"Yesterday," Kale replied.

"And we're just hearing about this now?" She faced the Blackmoors before returning her hooded gaze to Kale. "*We* should have been the ones you sought out with this information. *Not* the Blackmoors."

Kale stood taller, his golden eyes ablaze. "I don't answer to the Conclave. I serve the Beast King and no other."

His answer caused the Warlock Hag to flinch. When he had first arrived from Aeaea a few weeks ago, he'd been tentative and docile. That young shifter no longer existed.

Thad cleared his throat, and the hooded gazes of the entire Conclave settled on him. "Taking the Crests of the Five has been Icarian's game all along. We know that now." Thad stole a glance at the hooded figures in gray. One of them was Gerald, who had been Thad's closest confidant before he faked his death and ascended to the Conclave. Even though Thad still defended his decision of withholding information from his friend, the guilt still weighed upon him. "He wants the crests for this Spell Fall you mentioned on Aeaea."

"You must tell us what that means," Mr. Blackmoor pleaded. "If we know what we're up against, we may be able to stop it."

"Oliver is right." Gerald lowered his gray hood and took a step forward.

If the Warlock Hag had fur, it would have been bristling. She zoomed over to Gerald and floated before him. "You no longer serve as our voice. Return to the line at once."

Gerald waved her off before walking away. "I will not."

Everyone in the room gasped except the silent members of the Conclave, who merely observed.

The Warlock Hag disappeared, and one eyeblink later she barred Gerald's path. "Yes. You will."

Gerald regarded her for a few minutes, his gray eyes peering into the shadows of her hood while the rest of us waited in silence. Right now, they reminded me of two cowboys sizing each other up for a showdown at the O.K. Corral.

If they started tossing around their magic, someone might get killed in the crossfire.

"Stop!" I darted between them. It wasn't exactly the safest place to be, especially since I wasn't certain my magical immunity would hold out against power such as theirs. Still, I might be able to cancel out any stray spell just as I had been able to do with Sersie. "This is gettin' us nowhere."

A smile parted Gerald's lips. "Drake is correct." He patted my shoulder and winked. Perhaps the bridge between us hadn't been completely burned. "This infighting must end."

The Warlock Hag turned her hooded gaze to the rest of the Conclave. Silence consumed the room for several minutes as they held a discussion no one could hear. "Fine." She floated back to the others. "Have your conversation. We will have one of our own."

And with that, the other members of the Conclave blinked out of sight, leaving Gerald alone with us.

He glanced around the room, and the anger that had previously turned him against us no longer raged in his eyes. Gerald met all of our gazes, including Thad's, with the slanted grin of mischief he wore every time he confounded the other members of the Conclave. For an old wizard, he was quite the rebel. "I thought they'd never leave."

Thad immediately crossed over to Gerald. He reached out to touch his friend's shoulder but quickly withdrew his hand. He swallowed hard as if the words he was about to speak lodged themselves in his throat. "I'm sorry for lying to you, but even more than that." He bowed his head. "I'm even sorrier for not trusting you."

A huge smile spread across Gerald's lips as he rested his hands on Thad's shoulders. "Thank you for that, my friend. I know that wasn't easy."

The half smile that hitched up the right corner of Thad's lips revealed that it wasn't. Warlocks would rather be impaled than apologize.

"Excuse me!"

We all stared upward at Mason. After everything that had just happened, I'd completely forgotten he was even up there, and judging from the amused faces of most everyone else, so had they.

He crossed his arms over his chest and huffed. "Can someone get me the hell down now?"

SHORTLY AFTER Mason once again stood on the floor, Gerald took a seat and motioned for us to begin assaulting him with our questions.

"Will you tell us about the Spell Fall now?" Mr. Blackmoor asked.

"I will do my best to answer all your questions," he replied. "But first, I must say that the Conclave has… concerns with providing you this information. Even now, I can hear them bickering on the subject." Gerald rubbed his temples.

His answer intrigued me. For the first time since we met, Gerald hadn't said "we" when referring to the Conclave. "What do you think?" I asked.

Gerald settled his metallic gaze on me. "That we should have told you what we feared from the beginning."

"Then tell us," Mrs. Proctor urged. "Don't send us on any more missions with only half the information."

I locked eyes with Mason. The Proctors had been given a task, but no one was telling us what that was. The furrow in Mason's brow told me that bothered him as much as it did me.

In reply to Mrs. Proctor's question, Gerald took a deep breath and held it. What he decided next would have grave consequences. If he finally let us in on the secret, Gerald would be going against the Conclave, an act that might further fracture an already splintered group. If he didn't tell us what we needed to know, he placed all of us in even greater danger.

"The Spell Fall is an event of disastrous proportions and perhaps the deadliest curse in all of magic."

I couldn't believe my ears. From my time with the Blackmoors, I'd learned that the *immortalitas* spell, the magic responsible for creating Ben, the very first vampyre, was the only incantation that had been banned from all magical books across the community. What could be more horrible than that?

"It can't be worse that the *immortalitas* spell." Mason's words communicated my thoughts as if he could read my mind.

"But it is." Gerald lowered his gaze to his laced fingers in his lap. "By far."

My mouth went dry. Some nervously fidgeted with their clothes, while many just gazed at Gerald with surprise. Only Mr. Stonewall's expression remained the same. For the first time, I wished I could be as cold and logical as a wizard.

"What exactly happens after the Spell Fall?" he asked.

Gerald took a deep breath before squaring his shoulders and meeting our worried expressions. "The end of all magic."

A storm of questions blew through the room.

"Are you serious?"

"How is that possible?"

"Is there a way to stop it?"

"What can we do?"

That was a good question. How could we battle an enemy that might possess the power of the Conclave? Thinking about that made my head spin. I had to close my eyes and take deep breaths.

"What's the Conclave's plan?"

"Do you even know who Icarian is?"

"Is there a way to stop him?"

"What will happen to us?"

What would happen to Mason and his family if magic suddenly ended? What about the fae? They were made entirely of magic. If it suddenly disappeared, would the fae follow suit? Would Aiden just suddenly cease to exist? Would Kale and the shifters find themselves stuck in either their human or animal form?

I gritted my teeth. There were too many questions, too many terrifying possibilities, but the thing that bothered me the most was that no one was asking the *really* important question.

I marched up to Gerald and asked him what no one else had even thought to consider. "What possible reason could there be for such a spell to even exist?"

My question caused a bizarre expression to play across Mr. Stonewall's face. The single nod told me he was impressed, but did he have to look so shocked? I might not be magical, but I hadn't just fallen off the turnip truck.

"It was designed as a failsafe," Gerald replied. "To close the Gate should the situation ever warrant it."

"Why would anyone want to close the Gate?" Mr. Blackmoor rubbed his chin and glanced at Mr. Stonewall. "That doesn't make sense."

"But it does," Mr. Stonewall muttered. "Think about the state of our race at the beginning. We were at war with each other. Warlock fought witch and witch battled wizard. We killed each other for dominance, and it was our conflict that created the witch hunters."

"And they almost destroyed us." Thad stepped out of Aiden's arms, where he had sought comfort, and into the small circle that formed around Gerald. "Our species was out of control and headed toward extinction."

Gerald nodded. "And then our breeding with humans created the sorcerers."

"So the Spell Fall was created in the event that someone magical threatened all of life as we know it?" I asked.

"Precisely," Gerald said with a nod.

"This doesn't make sense." Mr. Stonewall placed his hands behind his back and stood straight. "If Icarian casts the Spell Fall and ends magic, he loses all the power he's gained. Why go through all this effort to acquire power just to have it taken away?"

Only one answer made sense to me. "He's scared."

"Of what?" Mason glanced around the room as the Stonewalls and Thad nodded.

"Who knows?" Thad shrugged. "But Icarian must be so afraid of something that he's willing to end all of magic to prevent it."

"I agree," Mr. Stonewall responded. "And we have to figure out what that is."

I turned to Gerald. "The Conclave created the crests for this very reason. Did they have any idea of what might be coming our way?"

Gerald shook his head. "No, they did not."

How could such a powerful group possess such little knowledge? It was extremely frustrating. "So how did the Conclave create the crests and where can we find the remaining two?"

Gerald settled back in his chair and sighed. "A spell that powerful needed talismans of equal strength, so the Conclave at that time siphoned energy directly from the Gate to create the Crests of the Five. Only with the talismans could the Spell Fall be cast, so the Conclave separated the crests and hid them all across the magical and human communities. Their locations were kept secret from other members of the Conclave, and though each subsequent Conclave knew of the Spell Fall and of the existence of the crests, only a select few had any knowledge where any of the crests were located. As an additional safeguard, no one member of the Conclave has ever known where all five were concealed. In fact, to my knowledge, the whereabouts of the Spirit Crest has remained a secret ever since it was first hidden."

Thad scratched his head. "So how can the Spell Fall be cast if no one knows where the last crest is?"

"The fifth crest can be found when the other four are joined together," Gerald replied.

This was a complicated mess, but considering the Spell Fall ended all of magic, making the spell easy would have been disastrous. While we might not know Icarian's motives or the location of the Spirit Crest, someone in the Conclave possessed information we needed. "Where is the Water Crest?" I asked.

Gerald regarded me with one arched silver eyebrow. "I cannot tell you that."

"But you know where it is?" Mr. Blackmoor asked.

"I do not." Gerald settled his gaze upon me before looking away. "I only had knowledge of the Earth Crest's location."

Yeah. It was the pendant he gave my aunt Millie, and possessing it had cost her her life. No matter how much he helped us now, I doubted I'd ever forgive him for that. "But someone on the Conclave knows where the Water Crest is?"

He took a deep breath before he nodded.

"Then why not tell us?" Mr. Stonewall asked. "If we can get to it before Icarian, we have the opportunity to stop the Spell Fall."

Gerald sighed. "If I possessed knowledge of its location, I would speak it."

"But you know which one of them does?" Thad asked.

His silence was his answer.

"Then summon the Conclave," Aiden commanded as if he was still the prince of the fire fairies. Gerald bristled at his tone, but Aiden didn't seem to notice. "Make him or her tell us where it is."

"Gerald cannot make me do anything," said a familiar metallic voice that suddenly echoed all around us. A second later the Conclave once again stood in our midst.

Of course the member of the Conclave who knew the location of the Water Crest was the one who hated us the most.

"I don't understand." Mr. Blackmoor took two tentative steps toward the Warlock Hag. "Why not simply provide us its location? We will retrieve it and return it to the Conclave. If you have the crest, Icarian won't be able to bring about the Spell Fall."

"We will no longer tell you anything." She floated over to Mr. Blackmoor and hovered over him like a wraith. "For far too many months, you have been allowed to spread doubt and insubordination like a plague. As such, the Conclave has decided to revoke your status as a protector coven for the Order of Black. The Edwells will serve in your stead."

Gerald stood, his fists shaking and his gray eyes turned harder than concrete. "No. This cannot be." He turned to face the unmoving robed figures. "We already discussed this."

"And we discussed it again," she replied with a dismissive wave. "Without *you*."

Mr. Blackmoor stepped forward, his jaw slack. All fight seemed to have left his body. "Please don't do this."

"We already have," she replied. "Your services are no longer needed or required."

A second later the world around us shimmered. When reality returned to normal, we no longer found ourselves in the Stonewalls' living room.

We were back home.

WE STOOD in the library in stunned silence. I didn't dare move or say a word. I'd been around warlocks long enough to know that the Blackmoors were on the verge of losing their tempers, and if they all went off at once, they could bring the house down around our ears.

Arcs of electricity fanned from Pierce's clenched fists, a frosty glare spread across Thad's hazel eyes, and the shadows coiled around Mason, but it wasn't their reaction I was most concerned with. It was Mr. Blackmoor's.

Not only could the man turn himself into stone and destroy everything in this house, but his magic was tied to his gestures. All it would take was one wave of his hand and the contents of this room would rise off the floor and slam into the walls.

I was surprised when all he did was let out a long sigh. "I'm going to bed." Without another word, he headed upstairs to his room and shut the door.

We gaped at each other for a few moments before storming up the stairs after him.

"Come on, Dad." Pierce leaned his bulky body against the frame of his father's shut door. "We can go back over to the Stonewalls' and make the Conclave listen."

Thad snorted. "That's suicide and you know it." He shouldered his way past Pierce and knocked on the bedroom door. "What we need to do is contact Gerald. He'll fight for us and get us reinstated. I know he will."

"Thad's right, Dad." Mason shoved Thad out of his way and pressed his face against the door. "We're the Blackmoor coven. Not only are we badass warlocks, but we've got a shifter, a vampyre fairy, and a human who's immune to magic. We've stopped a centuries-old vampyre-shadow weaver who could cast blood magic and was in league with a back-from-the-dead sorcerer and her mind-controlled army of shifters. We're not out of the game yet. Don't give up."

The door swung open, and Mr. Blackmoor studied the six of us. His high chin communicated his pride, as if he was not only ready but willing to carry through with their plans, but his tight shoulders communicated something else entirely. Mr. Blackmoor was terrified.

That wasn't the Oliver Blackmoor I knew. He didn't back away from a fight, and he wasn't afraid to do what was right even if it went against the norm. He'd demonstrated that when he accepted Aiden and me into his coven despite the protests of the protector covens and the Conclave.

So why was he so willing to turn tail and run now?

"I appreciate your dedication." He tousled Mason's thick black hair before settling his hands on Thad and Pierce's shoulders. "But the decision has been made. We are no longer a protector coven and are officially off this case."

"Then we can do it unofficially," Pierce prodded. "I know we can do it."

"And you wouldn't be alone," Kale said. "King Caspian longs for the return of his crown. He will provide us however many shifters we might need to face our mutual foe."

"I have no doubt, but the answer is no."

"But we can't do nothing, Mr. Blackmoor," Aiden said. "The fate of all magic is at stake."

"And that's precisely why we should have nothing more to do with this situation." His sudden resignation made sense. He'd fallen out of High Priest mode and switched to protective papa. "I'm trying to protect you. All of you. I've already lost your mother, and this family has faced enough danger to last several generations." His words caught in his throat, and it took him a few moments to regain his composure. "I don't know what I would do if I lost anyone else in this family."

Pierce draped his arm around his father's shoulders. "You won't lose us, Dad. We're tough. Just like you."

"That's right." Thad nodded as we all mimicked Pierce's move and stood in one unified circle, shoulder to shoulder. "We all are."

Mr. Blackmoor sniffled before letting out a frustrated laugh. "Fine."

Mason hooted while Pierce raised his hand to Thad for a high five. Thad glanced sideways at his brother and left him hanging.

"But we will do this on my terms. Understand me?" When he received nods from each one of us, he continued. "Pierce, I want you and Kale to search for spells to find the Water Crest. A talisman of that power is likely to emit magical energy of some kind. If we can find it, we can trace it."

"Will do," they said in unison.

He turned to Thad next. "I want you and Aiden to continue looking for Icarian. He's the key to ending all this. If we find him, we can stop the Spell Fall from ever happening."

"What about us?" Mason grabbed my hand and pulled me close, the light of anticipation dancing in his eyes. "What should we do?"

Mr. Blackmoor gripped Mason's face in his big hand and smiled down at him. "You, my son, have the most important job of all."

"What's that?" Mason asked, his voice shrill with excitement.

"Keep a low profile and stay out of the way."

Mason's jaw fell open, and even I did a double take.

"What the hell?" Mason asked. "Why?"

"Whatever Icarian's plan may be, it involves one or both of you. Aunt Millie's message is enough evidence of that. And as your High Priest and your father, it falls under my responsibility to protect you at all costs. You're to go to school, come home, and always stay together."

"But—"

Mr. Blackmoor locked his steely gaze upon Mason's. "You agreed to do this my way. Either all of you will follow my orders or I bench this entire family. I'll even bind your powers if I have to." He glared down at Mason. "The decision is yours."

Thad and Pierce both gave Mason a shove, to which he replied by scowling at them over his shoulder.

I took Mason's hand in mine and squeezed it. "We don't have any other choice."

Mason let out an exasperated sigh. "Fine."

"Good. Now everyone get to work." Mr. Blackmoor glanced down at the two of us. "And you two, get to bed. You've got school tomorrow."

Mason grumbled as his brothers and their boyfriends sprinted down the stairs to get started, but before I allowed Mason to pull me into our bedroom, I glanced over my shoulder at Mr. Blackmoor. His nod and smile told me he'd protect me, that he would make certain nothing happened to either Mason or me, so why did the wrenching in my gut tell me nothing Mr. Blackmoor or anyone could do would *ever* be enough?

That thought followed me into bed, and even though I settled into Mason's warm, naked embrace, I couldn't stop myself from shivering.

CHAPTER 6

I STOOD in the middle of a long, darkened hallway, clutching a pistol in one hand and a rapier in the other. Why the heck was I holding on to these weapons? And more importantly, where the heck was I?

My heart stopped pounding in my ears when I realized I had no answer.

The last thing I *did* remember was crawling into bed with Mason and then waking up here. Was this *another* dream?

It had to be, because I'd never been in this house before, and I'd certainly remember the black-and-brown mold dotting the ceiling and the unmistakable stench of rotting wood. Entryways to other rooms opened up to my left and right. I peered inside, scanning for the house's inhabitants or any signs of life, but the windows, covered in dirt and grime, only allowed in enough moonlight to paint a small patch of floor with a silvery, ethereal glow.

Long, deep shadows had claimed dominion over the rest of the real estate, sending their ebony arms toward the hallway as if challenging me to enter their domain.

Since my momma didn't raise a fool, that wasn't going to happen anytime soon.

Once again in the center of the corridor, I glanced over my shoulder at the front door, which stood open with a foot-sized hole in the frame.

No. It couldn't be. I slowly panned downward. When my tan-and-cream two-tone shoes came into view, I shuddered. I was in the house from my previous dream, and this gun and rapier were the blurry objects I'd been holding the last time. What the heck was going on?

A door begrudgingly creaked open behind me.

I spun around, squinting in the direction of the noise, trying to discern an advancing shape or the popping of wood under approaching footsteps. Only more darkness and silence greeted me. I stood completely still, holding the pistol with one trembling hand and pointing it at the void that stretched out before me.

That was when I took real notice of the gun. The silver grip resembled a dragon's claw. It seemed familiar, but why? Had I seen a picture of it in one of the many books in the Blackmoors' library? While that was definitely a possibility, since I'd read practically every book of their expansive collection, it didn't feel quite right.

The back of my brain itched as if something deep within the recesses of my memory were slowly clawing its way to the surface, and ice suddenly replaced my spine.

I shook my head, trying to force away the terror that squeezed my heart and refused to let go. I couldn't give in to my fear. If I did, I might never make it out of here and might never get back to Mason.

Images of his long dark hair, beautiful blue eyes, and slightly bronzed skin suddenly flashed in my mind. The memory of his musky, sweet scent soothed my rattled nerves, and when I recalled his warm kisses pressed against my lips, my neck, and all over my body, a wave of refreshing warmth spread across my chilled flesh and melted my ice-covered spine.

Mason had become my strength, my anchor. Whenever he touched me or looked at me, he made everything better. Apparently thinking about him had the same effect. Our love gave me the focus I needed.

Even though I had no clue where I was, I had a sneaking suspicion that magic was responsible for stealing me away from Mason's side. Was this some kind of attack?

A low, off-key whistle shredded the silence.

As if I'd been brandishing it my entire life, I cocked back the silver hammer on the pistol and aimed it at the darkness in front of me. I glanced over my shoulder and thrust the pointed blade into the gathering shadows that closed in behind me.

I held my breath and waited for my foe to appear.

"No matter how hard you try, you won't make it out of here alive."

The voice was both familiar yet foreign. I'd heard it before, but not with an English accent. Without thinking, I took a step forward, driven by a need to see my enemy before emptying the chamber of my pistol into his cold, corrupted heart.

But why did I want to kill him? Well, besides the fact that he obviously wanted to kill me?

Even though it felt like I'd entered a story already in progress, my finger involuntarily tensed against the trigger, and my jaw clenched. The answer became clear. I hated him. "I think you've got that backward, don't you?" My voice sounded deeper and more resonant than it had ever been. It reminded me of my father, but without the Texas twang. "I'll put a bullet in your head the moment I see your twisted grin."

A chuckle echoed all around me. "By the time you see me, you'll already be dead. Your weapons are nothing against my magic. We both know that."

Actually, we didn't both know that. Even though I had no clue what I was doing or what was going on, I did know one thing: I *did* have the power to kill him. He knew that as well as I did. "And we both know I'm more than just my weapons." What was I talking about?

"You're nothing compared to me or my kind." His voice rumbled like approaching thunder. "We're superior to you in every way imaginable. We have powers your pathetic mind could never comprehend. We evolved from you, and I won't rest until all humans are erased from this world."

I snorted. "And that's why you will die."

A cry of fury exploded from the shadows behind me. Before I had time to spin around, my enemy slammed into me, sending me sprawling across the floor and my weapons tumbling from my grasp. They skidded out of the hallway where we tussled and into the pitch-black room off to the right.

I had to get to them. If I didn't, I was a goner. My immunity to magic would be of no help. What made today different from when Sersie's spell passed harmlessly through me on Aeaea, or when Mrs. Proctor's attempt to erase my memories failed after I first learned of magic's existence?

The strong pair of hands that suddenly gripped my ankles told me I didn't have the luxury of finding the answer. My time was running out.

"*Incendere*." In response to the Latin word for *burn*, my flesh under his grip sizzled as magical flames sprouted from his palms.

I hollered in pain and spun around onto my back, wildly lashing out with my legs and kicking him in his face and chest.

He released his fiery grip, and the burning glow quickly died when his hands flew up to his face to stop the gush of blood that poured out of his nose. The shifting shadows in the corridor revealed only wisps of dark hair and one tanned fist, clenched in anger and pulsing with scarlet energy.

I scrambled backward, keeping my eyes trained on him and reaching into the darkened room for my weapons. He rose, removing his hands from his face, and pointed his fist at me. The magic at his command thrummed and pulsed, but as I closed my hand around the cool butt of the gun that would end this, his snarling expression came into view, made visible by the red glow of his power.

My breath caught in my throat, and my numb fingers could no longer feel the cool metal that would save my life. "Mason?"

A blinding flash of light filled my vision as more pain than I'd ever experienced ripped through my gut.

"Drake, are you okay?"

I jumped at the voice at my side and scrambled to my right, falling off the bed and landing with a painful thud on the cold wooden floor. The world suddenly spun around me, and everything went white.

"Shit, Drake." Mason scrambled to my side of the bed and looked down at where I lay. "What's wrong?"

I scurried away from him, fearful that he would once again try to kill me. When he ran his hand through the tangled mess of his black hair and his sleep-weary face broadened into the kind smile that always melted my butter, the jackhammer that had become my heart returned to a normal rhythm.

I glanced around the room. The dark hallway was gone, and the weapons I'd been carrying were nowhere to be seen.

What the hell was going on?

"Drake?"

Mason suddenly crouched next to me. Concern hooded his blue eyes as he ran the back of his hand across my cheek. I held my breath, waiting for his baby blues to narrow at me with hatred. When he pressed his lips to my cheek, my guard dropped, and I fell into his embrace, shaking like a newborn fawn.

"It was just a dream." Mason kissed the top of my head and pulled me close. "Just a dream."

I buried my face in Mason's chest, burrowing as deep into his loving arms as I could. But no matter how much I wanted him to be right, the dread that filled my stomach told me he was wrong.

That was no dream.

EVEN AFTER fifteen minutes in Mason's comforting embrace, I still felt colder than a cast-iron commode. No matter how hard I clung to him or how many times he kissed my forehead, nose, or lips, I kept waiting for him to suddenly start speaking in an English accent and want to kill me.

"Don't worry." He pulled me even tighter against him, as if he could sense my turmoil. "It's over now."

But was it? My trembling body sure didn't know that. Even in Mason's secure embrace, the fear from my dream, or whatever the hell that was, clung to my soul like ice crystals. Instead, snaking tendrils of chill spread across my flesh.

"Are you cold?"

"No, just...."

He brushed my hair out of my face and kissed the tip of my nose. "Just what?"

Terrified, confused, worried, and a whole bunch of other emotions that couldn't be named. It was like Pandora's box had been opened inside me.

"You just don't feel safe right now."

God, he knew me so well. I *didn't* feel safe, even though there was no place safer than in the arms of the boy I loved inside a house filled with warlocks, a vampyre fairy, and a shifter. This place was a magical Fort Knox, but that knowledge didn't erase the impending sense of danger.

Mason nuzzled into my neck, his warm breath fanning across my flesh. "Well, I'm not going anywhere and I'd never let anything happen to you. You know that."

Part of me did, but a tiny drop of doubt had fallen into the ocean of love and security Mason had filled my life with, which didn't make a damn bit of sense. The Mason who held me now could never be the Mason from that nightmare, because that was all it was—a nightmare.

What else could it have been?

"Better?"

I repositioned myself in Mason's embrace, resting my head on his shoulder and gazing up at the complete adoration shining down on me. "I'm gettin' there."

Mason smiled before running his fingers over my mouth. "Good." He leaned forward and pressed his lips to mine. "Want to talk about it?"

If I never had to think about that dream again, it would be much too soon. "I'd rather not. It was awful."

"Are you sure? Sometimes it's better to talk them out. I've had some experience with bad dreams, you know?"

That Mason did. He had been plagued with nightmares before we met, and they turned out to be omens that Ebenezer Kane was on his way to Havenbridge to try to kill Mason and his family, but there was no way my dream could be some portent of doom.

I wasn't a warlock, and there wasn't anything magical about me. Well, besides my immunity to magic. That was a mystery that sure needed to be solved once and for all.

"Drake?"

Mason's voice brought me out of my thoughts and back to the warm arms around me. "No. I don't want to talk about it."

"But—"

I moved from lying in his arms to straddling him on the floor. A different kind of shiver tore through my body as I pressed my ass onto his groin. "I said no."

Mason grabbed my hips as I undulated on top of him and pressed my lips to his forehead, his cheeks, and finally his mouth. "What are you doing?"

"What does it look like I'm doin'?" My words came out low and rough as I licked a trail from Mason's mouth to his sensitive neck.

He groaned, arching his hips up against me. "Drake—"

I pressed my finger to his lips and shushed him. I didn't need or want to talk about my dream right now. What my body and my soul required was Mason's skin on mine. My flesh called out for his hands to slide over me and down my ass. I longed for his lips upon my aching hardness and his tongue invading my mouth. I needed to feel the weight of his body on top of me, filling me with a renewing rain of love that would flush away all the negative emotions my nightmare had stirred up.

"Stop." He placed one hand on my chest and gently pushed me away. "I love making love to you more than just about anything. You know that. But you just had a nightmare, most likely brought on by your grief, by everything that's happened. You haven't processed it all yet.

What you need is rest, to fall asleep in my arms, to know I will always keep you safe."

His concern sent a wave of desire into my groin. "What I need is you." I fell upon his lips, whimpering at the hardness growing underneath me. My soul and my heart might be heavy, but not as weighty as the overwhelming urgency that consumed me in a flash fire of passion.

The low, guttural growl that vibrated in his chest and in his kiss made me smile. He cupped my chin as he tenderly broke from our kiss and forced me to gaze deeply into his blue eyes. He slipped his free hand beneath the waistband of my shorts and grabbed my cock. "Are you sure this is what you want?" He slowly jacked my shaft, squeezing firmly at the base before sliding his grip up and around the leaking crown.

I moaned in response, grinding myself harder onto his erection.

He pounced on my lips, fluttering his insistent fingers down my shaft and toward my balls. Whenever he did that, I lost the ability to think. I abandoned the fear that crawled with me and gave myself over to Mason's wonderful wandering fingers as they danced around my entrance.

"You haven't answered my question."

How could I when Mason slipped a finger into my body? Each circle he drew inside me drove me wild and turned my breathing ragged. "Yes. I want this. I want you." My voice was low and breathy as he jacked my dick harder and faster. I leaned against Mason, giving myself over to the rhythmic pulses his fingers sent rippling through me.

Mason hummed, kissing my ear and my neck as his hands continued to cast his magic upon my sizzling flesh. "That's all I needed to hear."

He supported my butt with one hand while he used the other to give him the leverage he needed to stand. I wrapped my legs around his waist, and after a straining grunt, he rose before turning around and leaning me back onto the bed. With one tug, he yanked the shorts I slept in from my body and stared down at my nakedness.

I sat up, delivering butterfly kisses to his flat stomach while I dipped my fingers beneath the fabric of his shorts before sliding them off his hips. As always when I saw him naked, my breath hitched at the lean muscles that rippled across his smooth, tanned skin, the strong, squared shoulders, the slim waist, the swell of his cock that sprouted out of a light dusting of jet-black hair.

I pressed my nose to his skin and inhaled, taking in the scent of musk, sweat, and cinnamon soap that clung to the air around him. The aroma drove me to bury my face in his groin, lapping at his salty flesh before taking him in my mouth.

"Holy shit!" Mason gasped and wound his fingers through my hair. He thrust his hips forward, shoving his length down my throat. I circled my tongue along his shaft as he eased himself in and out of my mouth. When the salty sweetness of precum fell onto my tongue, my hunger for Mason intensified. I slurped it up, grabbed his ass, and forced myself to the base.

Having Mason inside me and hearing the whimpers and moans my mouth and tongue ripped from his body filled the chasm that had briefly opened in my stomach. The gnawing fear subsided, replaced by the overpowering love and desire that filled the room with heavy breathing and the musky cloud of sex.

"You've got to stop." Mason held my shoulders and gently eased himself from my lips.

"Why?" I grabbed his cock, twirling my tongue around the head and along the slit to drink up more of his sweetness. "I'm not done."

"Yeah, well, I will be if you keep that up." He leaned forward, pressing his lips to mine. As our tongues danced around the slick sweetness that coated my kiss, Mason grabbed my shoulders before forcing me onto the mattress. "It's your turn."

I crawled backward on the bed, allowing room for Mason to join me. He slid between my parted legs, leaving soft kisses on my inner thighs that sent shivers across my flesh. He nibbled and licked a trail up my goose-pimpled flesh until he danced his tongue across my sac. "Oh," I managed to force out as Mason swallowed my prick.

He held the base firmly as he slid eagerly up and down, coating my shaft with the spit he used to jack and suck me at the same time. When he lapped his tongue around the sensitive tip, I clawed at the sheets. When he slid down to the hilt, I almost blacked out. He continued that sensuously torturous motion for several more minutes, bringing me just seconds away from a soul-shattering orgasm.

Right before I fell over the precipice, Mason allowed me to slip from his pursed lips. "Not yet."

"Wh-why not?"

In response, Mason hoisted my legs over his shoulders and dove into my crevice. I cried out as he lapped his probing tongue around my opening, slipping it inside before pulling out and dancing around the rim. He was driving me crazy. If I didn't have him inside me soon, I was going to crawl out of my skin.

"Please, Mason. I need you... so... so bad."

"How bad?" He slipped a finger inside, loosening me up for what I needed most.

I trembled around the intruding digit. "*Real* bad."

A hoarse growl escaped his throat as he shoved two more fingers inside. He scissored them several times before adding a third. I practically levitated off the bed from the magic he cast within and across my shuddering body. I had to cover my face with a pillow to keep from screaming out in pleasure. A second later the nightstand rumbled open and the cap of the lube bottle clicked.

I tossed the pillow aside to watch Mason coat his cock.

"Are you ready?"

Was he serious? I was shaking with need and panting like a bulldog in a Texas heat wave. "*So* ready."

With my trembling legs resting on Mason's shoulders, he pressed himself at my entrance and leaned forward. The swollen head of his shaft slid past the rim as he filled me, until there was no longer anything between us.

"You feel so good," he mumbled against my skin as he kissed my throat, my chin, and my lips.

I gasped as he slid in and out with one forceful stroke. "Oh, Mason. This is what I needed."

Mason held himself above me, using the leverage to force himself harder and faster inside me. I shoved my hand between us, jacking my prick to the rhythmic beats of Mason's thrusts until our strokes were in synch. The combined sensation sent shudders traveling across my flesh, down my spine, and around my cock and ass as they were overstimulated by the intensity of the pleasure.

I rocked my hips upward against him, further electrifying the current that passed between our bodies. "Make love to me. Show me there's no reason to be afraid."

Mason held me tight in his arms, pressing his forehead to mine. "No reason... to ever... be afraid," he grunted. "I'm with you... always."

His words and my lube-slick hand ripped the orgasm out of my body, sending jets of semen splattering across my stomach. My convulsing body sent Mason over the edge. With one final grunt, he shoved himself to the hilt, triggering his own climax.

I wrapped my arms and legs around him, trying to draw him completely inside, where I needed him most, and for several minutes, we lay there, catching our breath and reveling in the slick sweat of our exhausted bodies.

"Drake." He whispered my name before slipping out of me and sliding off. He drew me into his arms, pressing my damp body against his. "I love you, and whatever it was about your dream that scared you, I need you to remember that you're not alone, that no matter what happens, you and I will face it together."

And that was exactly what my sighing soul needed. Whatever my dream was or might mean, it didn't have the power to rob me of what was real and true, and this, right here, was my reality. Against that, nothing else mattered.

"I love you, Mason."

He kissed the back of my neck and sheltered me in his arms. "And I love you too."

I drifted off to sleep, confident and strong once again.

CHAPTER 7

A SUCCESSION of loud bangs jolted me awake. I sat up, pulled open the nightstand drawer, and reached inside for the pistol I kept there for times such as these. When my hand didn't close around the cool silver butt of the gun, I panicked. Where the hell was it?

"Fuuuuck!" Mason groaned in bed next to me. "Leave us alone."

"Get your lazy asses out of bed. We've got shit to do."

It was Pierce on the other side of the door, not—

Not who?

Mason sat up, flipped off the closed door, and burrowed back under the covers.

Pierce banged on the frame three more times. "I mean it. Get your asses downstairs in fifteen minutes or Dad'll be the one coming up here to get you."

Crap. We definitely didn't want that. Mr. Blackmoor didn't tolerate tardiness. He'd transform his body into stone and turn the bedroom door into splinters. "We'll be right down."

Pierce grunted before his footsteps padded back downstairs.

I nudged Mason with my foot. "Wake up."

"Can't. Tired. Need sleep."

What I needed was answers. There was definitely more to that dream from last night.

"Mason, please. We need to talk."

A low snore was my only reply.

"Somethin's wrong."

He sat up as if he were a jack-in-the-box. Even though his eyes were still half-closed and his black hair resembled a rat's nest, the hum of his shadow powers filled the room. "Who is it? What is it? Tell me where to shoot."

I sighed before placing a reassuring hand on his shoulder. "Jeez. Power down before you blast me." The hateful gaze of the Mason in my dream filled my memory. I shook the image from my mind and took several deep breaths.

"Did you have that dream again?"

"I don't think it was a dream."

He scrunched up his lips and glanced sideways at me. "Then what the hell was it?"

That was the million-dollar question. "That's what we need to find out."

"Okay. Then tell me exactly what happened in your dream."

As Mason and I got ready for whatever Mr. Blackmoor had planned for the day, I filled him in on the dream. When I was done, he stared at me with his toothbrush hanging out of his mouth. "You dreamed I tried to kill you?" The mouthful of toothpaste garbled his words.

"Yes, but I don't think it was the real you."

He spat in the sink and rinsed his mouth. "What the hell does that even mean?"

I wasn't entirely certain, but my gut told me that was as close to an answer as I was going to get right now. "I don't really know. It seemed to be you, but you talked with an English accent and you weren't a shadow weaver."

Mason crossed over to his closet, took out a black, hooded shirt, and pulled it on. "You said my hands glowed red?"

"Yeah," I answered as I finished pulling up my jeans. "What kind of power is that?"

He sat down on the bed to put on his socks and shoes. "Could be a lot of things, since warlocks get their active powers by combining two of the five magical elements. Are you sure the me in your dream was even a warlock? You could've been fighting a witch like Mr. Proctor, who can project fire."

"But it wasn't fire he shot at me. His hands turned to flames in response to a spell he cast. His active power wasn't fire. It was red energy."

Mason nodded. "Okay, then it had to be a warlock, but I'm not certain what type of warlock abilities are associated with red energy. We'd have to ask either Dad or Thad."

I grabbed my blue-and-gray sweater and pulled it on. "No. We can't."

"What? Why not?"

I wasn't certain of that answer either, but my gut told me this was something we had to ferret out on our own. Judging from Mason's rigid stance, though, I was going to have to give him some semblance of a reasonable answer, and there was only one I could think of. "They're too busy tryin' to find Icarian and the Water Crest. We can't afford to distract them, not with the fate of all magic on the line. This is somethin' we're goin' to have to do ourselves."

"But we promised Dad we wouldn't get involved and stay out of their way."

Although Mason didn't mind breaking promises he'd made to people outside the coven, when it came to his family, his word meant everything to him. It was one of the many reasons I loved him. "I know, and we'll keep that promise. This has nothin' to do with Icarian or the Spell Fall." At least I hoped so. "This has everythin' to do with me, and maybe it can help explain what Aunt Millie told us or even my immunity to magic."

A grin hitched up the corners of his lips. "You know, I'm rubbing off on you."

He evidently meant that as a compliment, but since Mason typically acted rashly and ticked off pretty much everyone he came into contact with, I wasn't too certain I felt the same. "What does that mean?"

He rubbed his thumb along my jawline before planting a big smack on my lips. "You're getting sneakier every day." He grabbed my hand and tugged me toward the door. "Come on. I've got an idea."

AFTER MASON tugged me down the stairs and into the kitchen, where sizzling bacon made the room smell like heaven, he grabbed two protein bars from the pantry and shoved them into my hands.

What the hell was this? It was Saturday morning, and my watering mouth and grumbling stomach wanted my usual mountain-sized portion of bacon, not a cardboard-flavored snack.

Mason rolled his eyes at my pinched expression before grabbing my hand and yanking me toward the back door.

"And just where do you two think you're going?"

Mr. Blackmoor's words froze us in our tracks.

Mason took one tentative step forward. "Out?"

"Try again," he said, waving the greasy spatula at the both of us.

"Aw, come on, Dad. You're the one who benched us, who told us not to get in your way. That's what we're trying to do."

Mr. Blackmoor shot Mason a blank stare, obviously not believing one word. He then shifted his gaze to me. "We're just takin' your advice and getting' out from underfoot."

He ran his fingers through his hair and sighed. "The two of you are up to something. I know it."

"When *isn't* Mason up to something?" Thad asked as he and Aiden entered the room. From their bleary, bloodshot eyes, the two of them had been up all night researching spells that would help them locate Icarian.

Mason sniffed. "It's nice to know how highly my family thinks of me."

"It's actually a lot lower than you might imagine." Pierce stood behind us with sweat dripping down his bare chest. He'd either been in his room working out or engaged in some other physical activity with Kale, who trailed along behind him.

Kale bumped his shoulder into Pierce's arm. His wide eyes and big smile gave me the answer I didn't really need. "Don't be so mean."

"Listen to your boyfriend, Pinkie."

Everyone chuckled at Mason's comment while Pierce scowled. Ever since Pierce put an end to Ben and Sersie on Aeaea by turning into pink lightning, Mason had taken great pleasure in teasing him about the color of his new and extremely deadly power.

"Or what?" Pierce took two steps.

I stood in between them. "Will the both of y'all just stop?"

Pierce and Mason pointed at each other and said, "He started it."

"That's enough!" Mr. Blackmoor's order was instantly followed by silence. "With everything we have to deal with, can we please suspend the brotherly put-downs for one morning?"

"Not a problem." Mason grabbed my hand and shouldered past Pierce, who growled at him. "We're heading out for a few hours."

"Think again." Mr. Blackmoor pointed to us and then to the stools at the bar. "The two of you are going to put your butts in those chairs or I'm going to cast a barrier spell that will prevent you from putting one toe outside these walls."

I had no doubt he'd do it, and neither did Mason. He complained as he stomped over to the bar like a five-year-old and fell into his seat in a huff. I took the stool next to him and arched my eyebrows. What were we going to do now?

Mason's slanted lips told me he wasn't down for the count yet. "So you're just going to keep us prisoner here?"

Mr. Blackmoor returned his attention to the bacon. "If that's what it takes to keep you both safe, then yes."

"Okay, then." Mason spun around in his seat and faced Thad. "So what have you found?"

Thad eyed him over his glass of orange juice. "I might be able to piece together an incantation from other spells that hopefully will lead us to Icarian."

"Cool. What are the spells?"

"Why do you care?"

Mason leaned onto the counter and gave Thad his full attention. He rarely did that. "Just curious. Since you're always saying I should learn more about magic, I figured this was as good a time as any. What spells are you going to combine?"

"Well—"

"And how do you plan on doing that? I mean, only really powerful warlocks are capable of creating their own spells."

Thad nodded. "Yes, but I did it before on—"

"Otherworld. Yeah, you told us that a few months ago. How *did* you do that? Did you ever figure that out? I mean, you said you were going to, but you never told us that you did."

Thad's hazel eyes narrowed and the apples of his fair cheeks scorched red.

"So did you figure it out and not tell us? If so, why keep it a secret?"

Thad opened his mouth to answer, but Mason rambled on.

"The other option is you never figured it out and you didn't tell us. Is that because you don't want us to think you're not as smart as you like to think you are?"

Pierce rubbed the bridge of his nose. "Will you let him answer?"

"And what about you?" Mason set his sights on Pierce now. "Have you discovered a way to find the Water Crest? If you did, how did you manage to get around whatever protection spell the Warlock Hag most likely cast to prevent it from being detected?"

Pierce scrunched up his lips. He obviously hadn't considered that angle.

"And another thing—"

"Dad?" Thad crossed over to the stove and placed his hand on his father's increasingly tense shoulders. "Maybe letting Mason and Drake out of the house for a few hours will do us all some good."

A slight grin hitched up the corners of Mason's mouth. He might be irritating, but he was also a genius.

Mr. Blackmoor shook his head. "It's too dangerous."

"But they'll be together. They can keep each other safe, and they'll keep their cell phones on and with them the entire time." Thad glanced over his shoulder at us. "Isn't that right?"

"Of course," we answered in unison.

Mr. Blackmoor's stern expression revealed he was just about to say no for the final time, when Thad quickly intervened. "Besides, there are some ingredients we're out of, and I need them for my spell. Mason and Drake can collect them and then come right back."

"We'd be glad to." Our voices once again came out as one.

Through gritted teeth, Mr. Blackmoor answered, "Fine." He pointed at the both of us. "Get what Thad needs and bring your asses back here right away. Understood?"

I rose from my seat. "Yes, sir."

Instead of replying, Mason stood up and saluted. Even when he won, he pushed the boundaries.

Mr. Blackmoor placed eight pieces of bacon in a paper towel and handed them to us. "Now get out of here before I change my mind."

Mason and I nodded quickly before darting out the kitchen door. We were halfway across the lawn toward the back entrance to the garage when Thad screamed at us from the back porch. "Don't you want the list?"

I spun around and smacked my head. "Yeah, I guess that'll be somewhat useful."

"Let me send it." Thad took out his phone and typed on the screen. When he was done, Mason's phone chimed.

Mason opened his phone and gave his brother a thumbs-up. "We got it."

"Good." Thad crossed over to where we stood, a devious smile dangling from his lips. "You two have a few hours to collect everything on that list *and* accomplish whatever it is you're both up to."

Mason opened his mouth to speak, but he only succeeded in mimicking a fish out of water. I didn't fare any better. I couldn't even get my lips to move.

"And don't either of you dare deny it." He settled his hazel gaze on Mason. "Only desperation would drive someone to be as annoying as you were just now. I assume this has something to do with Aunt Millie."

In a way, it did—my dreams hadn't started until after my run-in with her—so I nodded.

"I thought so." He arched an eyebrow at Mason. "And will you be breaking our promise to Dad?"

Mason chewed on his lower lip, clearly unsure how to answer. "I don't think so."

"You had better not." He poked Mason in the chest. "I'm taking a big chance letting you both out of this house, considering everything, but you've both proven capable of handling yourselves." The tension painting his voice gave way to concern. "I know how important getting answers about your aunt Millie is to you, and if it helps us out, I'm all for it."

"Thanks, Thad." I gave him a hug.

He patted my back. "Don't either of you make me regret this. Promise me you'll both be safe and you'll stay together."

"We will." Mason grabbed my hand and tugged me forward a few steps before he stopped and glanced over his shoulder at his brother. "And thanks."

A few seconds later, we climbed into Mason's car and sped away.

"SO WHERE exactly are we goin'?" I asked as Mason broke several traffic laws getting us to downtown Havenbridge.

He brought the car to a jerking halt and gestured to the building to my right.

"Starbucks? What help about my dreams could we possibly get here?"

"O ye of little faith." He exited the car and waved at the store's interior. "Who comes here every day like clockwork?"

One glance through the window answered his question. Mason was a genius, not that I'd ever admit that. I'd never hear the end of it if I did. Instead I pressed a kiss to his lips and led him through the door and toward Miranda and Charlotte, who stood off to the side, waiting for their order.

Miranda scowled as she saw us approach. "And I was having such a good day."

"You're no ray of sunshine either," Mason said with a smirk.

Miranda grabbed her sister's hand. "You asked us to wait for you here, and against my better judgment, we did." I gaped at Mason. When had he done that? "That was a mistake," she said before turning around.

"Miranda, wait!" I blocked their path. Even though I was still upset at them for keeping secrets from us, I couldn't hold it against them, not when they were following orders. Besides, we needed their help. "We really need to talk to you."

Charlotte, who was always the first to melt at an apology, smiled and gave me a big hug. "Okay, we'll stay."

Miranda scowled at Mason. "I'll stay if Roach Boy apologizes."

Oh good Lord. Would this madness never end? Miranda and Mason knew exactly what buttons to push for maximum carnage. For two people who didn't like each other, they were two peas in a pod.

"We don't have time for this. We really need your help."

The pleading tone in my voice got Charlotte's attention. She led us to a corner table, and we all sat down. "What happened? Is it about your aunt Millie?"

"Kinda." Mason glanced over his shoulder, making sure no one was in earshot. "Tell us what's going on. What don't we know?"

Charlotte did a double take. "Are you out of your mind? You know the rules. I can only discuss protector coven business with other members of the protector covens."

Mason flinched. "Really? If that was true, you should have told us about the secret mission the Conclave sent you on. We were still a protector coven, or maybe you didn't because you already knew the Edwells replacing us was a done deal. I thought we were friends, Charlotte. Friends help each other, and they don't let them get blindsided." Resentment poisoned his tone and brought a slight flush to his cheeks.

"I know you feel betrayed, but we didn't know for sure the Edwells would replace you. We figured they might after what happened on Aeaea." Charlotte fidgeted with the threads on the sleeve of her white angora sweater and refused to meet our gazes. "I'm sorry for that. I really am. It's not like we wanted that to happen or even asked for it."

The red in Mason's cheeks spread across his face. "Bull! Your parents couldn't have been happier, and the Stonewalls? They practically danced a jig when that Warlock Hag made the announcement."

Miranda's narrowed eyes met Mason's. "And you wonder why you were replaced? You don't treat the members of the Conclave with respect. You continue to defy them in actions and words. Look where that got your family."

"And where has blindly following them got your family? You know the Edwells don't have the power the Blackmoors do. What's going to happen when and if you face Icarian?"

Her shoulders tensed in response to Mason's comment. It was obviously something she had already considered. "Your family is more at risk now than they were before."

Charlotte's long sigh communicated her agreement. "And what would you have me or my family do? Openly challenge the Conclave as well?"

"It would be a start," Mason replied with a sniff.

Miranda snorted while Charlotte crossed her arms and huffed. This was getting us nowhere. I had to appeal to Charlotte's previous concerns. She hadn't agreed with anything the Conclave had said or done. Although it was a long shot, since Charlotte typically followed orders to a T, we needed our friends, not the mindless drones the Conclave preferred. "Please. We need your help. Somethin' bad is comin' to Havenbridge, and it's not just Icarian or the Spell Fall."

Her mouth fell open and she touched her parted lips. "How did you find out?"

Miranda gaped at her sister while Mason grabbed my knee under the table and gave it a triumphant squeeze. I had bluffed, and it had worked. I *was* becoming just as sneaky as my warlock. God help me!

"We'll show you ours if you show us yours," Mason said with his standard cocky grin.

Miranda rose from the table and pulled her sister to a standing position. "We'll be back. I need a word with my sister." She led Charlotte toward the restrooms.

Even though they hadn't decided to help us yet, my gut told me they would, so I let out the breath I hadn't even realized I'd been holding. Perhaps we would finally get some answers.

WHILE CHARLOTTE and Miranda talked in the restroom, Mason stood in line to order some drinks. I'd been lost in thought, wondering what information Charlotte and Miranda possessed, when a hand suddenly waved in front of me. Will stood beside me, flashing his pearly whites while shaking his long sandy-blond hair out of his beanie. "I've been calling to you for like five minutes." He slid into the seat across from me, and I tensed. Will couldn't be here. We had important matters to discuss. "What were you doing? Remembering your last pumpkin spice latte?"

I kicked him under the table.

"Ow! That fucking hurt."

"Good. You were bein' a jerk."

"Maybe." He rubbed his leg and sneered at me. "But that's no reason to get violent."

"Aw, does the widdle baby have an owie?"

Will flipped me off with a smile. "You're an ass. We're gonna get along just fine."

Maybe when I didn't have a magical mystery to solve. "So what are you doin' here besides givin' me a hard time?"

He nodded to his dad, who stood to the left of the baristas' station waiting for his order. With any luck, they'd get their drinks and leave.

"So I need to ask you something."

Will's words recaptured my attention. "What is it?"

"You know any banging chicks you could introduce me to? I'm in desperate need of a bae, preferably one with a big booty."

I chuckled. "So you like big booties, huh?"

He rubbed his hands together. "I love them! You know any girls with more cake than a bakery shop?"

I did and her name was Miranda Proctor. "Maybe."

Will sat on the edge of his seat. "How big are we talking? Like Kim Kardashian big?"

I rolled my eyes. "No."

"But she's got a big ass, right? Is she hot? Do you have a picture? Do you think she'd go out with me?"

"You need to calm down before I turn the hose on you."

"Fuck, man. Don't leave a bro hanging." If Will salivated any more, I'd have to grab a mop.

"Her name is Miranda Proctor."

"Have I met her?"

"Nope. She's been absent the past few days." I pulled out my phone and showed him a picture Miranda and I took during Yule.

"Man, she is fine." He leaned back in his chair and studied the ceiling. Whatever he was imagining in his head, I wanted no part of.

"Straight boys are weird."

His right eyebrow arched so far across his forehead it was like he'd gotten a fishhook stuck in it. "Hey, man. I'm cool with the gay thing, so if you're gonna be my friend, you're gonna have to be cool with the straight thing."

"I suppose I could put up with it as long as we leave the girly bits out of our conversations."

"If you're willing to not talk about Mason's junk, I'm all in."

Will held out his hand, and I took it. "Deal."

"And what type of bargain did you two just strike?" Mr. Hopkins stood next to us with two beverages in his hand. He handed one to Will before pulling up a chair and joining us.

"We were just talking, Dad." The light of merriment quickly drained from Will's eyes once Mr. Hopkins sat down. They were supposed to leave, not make themselves comfortable. What was I going to do now?

"So I heard." He took a sip of his coffee before studying us. "What's the subject of guy talk these days?"

There was something about the tone of his voice I didn't like. It reminded me of a gauntlet being thrown. "I'm not sure you'd find it very interestin', Mr. Hopkins."

He regarded me over his cup. "And why's that?"

"We were talkin' about Mason, my boyfriend."

His lip curled slightly before he stretched it out into a smile. "That boy I saw you with after school yesterday?"

"That's the one."

"You two seemed… close."

Why did he say that if it was a bad thing? There was only one reason I could think of. "Do you have a problem with gay people?" My tone was razor-sharp, but I didn't care. After everything I'd been through, I wasn't going to put up with a homophobic prick.

Will's lower jaw practically unhinged. He darted his gaze between his father and me, apparently uncertain what to do or say.

Mr. Hopkins leaned back in his chair, locking his crisp blue gaze upon mine. I didn't flinch and didn't look away. After a few seconds, a smile broke across his stony expression. "Not at all." He took a sip of his coffee, which was still hot judging by the slight grimace. "A good friend of mine in the Marines was homosexual."

Why didn't I believe him? There was something about my relationship with Mason he didn't like.

"I won't lie, though. Whenever I see kids as young as yourself so comfortable with your sexuality and boldly displaying it for others, it surprises me. That just wasn't how things were done in my day."

"But it's how we do things now."

He held up his coffee to me. "You're right. Life is all about change, whether we're ready for it or not."

What exactly did he mean by that?

Before I had a chance to ask, Mason sidled up to the table, glancing back and forth between Will and his father before handing me my drink. "Here's your hot chocolate."

Mr. Hopkins held out his hand to Mason. "You must be Drake's boyfriend. I'm Flint Hopkins, Will's dad."

"Nice to meet you, Mr. Hopkins. I'm Mason." He took Mr. Hopkins's hand and offered him the big, toothy smile he reserved for people he didn't like.

Mr. Hopkins stood up and nodded at Will. "We should hit the road."

"I'm gonna hang here for a bit." He locked his wide, pleading eyes with mine. "If that's okay?"

Mason gripped my shoulder tightly. It was his way of reminding me we had magical business to complete. Even though he was right, I couldn't be rude. "No problem."

Mr. Hopkins took in Mason's rigid posture before turning to me. "Are you sure?"

I took Mason's hand in mine and held it tight. It was my way of telling him we'd figure this out. "Yes. We'll even give him a ride home."

"Really?" If Will were any more surprised, he'd have just won the lottery.

Mason let out a sigh and nodded, accepting that my mind had been made up. "Sure."

"Well, okay, then. See you boys later." Mr. Hopkins gave us a salute before turning around and sauntering out the door like a man who'd gotten exactly what he wanted.

CHAPTER 8

"So how are we gonna ditch him?" Mason asked, glancing over his shoulder at Will, who stood in line to order another beverage.

I took a sip of my hot chocolate before answering. "How long have you known me?"

"We're not ditching him?"

"There you go," I said with a grin.

Mason banged his head on the table two times before sitting up straight and running his fingers through his long dark locks. "How the hell are we supposed to do what needs to be done with that jerk hanging around?"

Will wasn't a jerk. He was a kid going through a rough time that most likely had something to do with his father. More than anyone else, Mason knew what that was like. When we first met, he and his father had been butting heads nonstop. "You could be a bit more compassionate, you know."

Mason's bushy eyebrows arched so high over his forehead, they joined his hairline. "What are you talking about? I didn't turn Will into a cockroach when he called me an idiot yesterday. I'd say that's being pretty damn compassionate."

I loved Mason, but sometimes you needed a two-by-four to get a point across. "He's havin' a tough time, Mason. He's new here and things between him and his father are tense. Plus, he's never mentioned his mother." I paused to let that sink in.

"Oh." His eyes turned glassy and faraway. Mason still hadn't recovered from his mother's death the year before, and whether Will lost his mom due to death or divorce, both Mason and I understood firsthand what someone went through after such a devastating loss. "Fine. I'll stop giving him a hard time."

There was the boy I loved.

"But if he gives me shit, I'm still gonna knock him on his ass."

And there was the warlock I loved. Separating the two was impossible, but I wouldn't have him any other way. I laced my fingers with his and pressed a kiss to his lips. "If he gives you shit, I'll knock him on his ass for you."

A big grin stretched across his face. "I love you too."

Will cleared his throat, standing at the table, most likely unsure whether he should sit or give us some privacy. When Mason pushed the chair away from the table with his foot, Will accepted the invitation with a beaming smile and sat down. "Thanks again for letting me hang with you for a bit. My dad has been driving me crazy, and I needed some space."

Mason chuckled. "Man, I know how that goes. My dad and brothers give me shit all damn day, every day of my life. It sucks."

"Yeah." Will stared at the lid of his coffee and nodded. "Listen, I know you two have shit to do, so I won't crowd you. I'll just finish my coffee and jet."

Mason waved off his words. "No worries. We're here with some friends."

Will glanced around. "Are they invisible?"

They might as well be. Charlotte and Miranda had been in the restroom for what felt like forever. I nodded to the back where the women's room was. "Nope. They're indisposed."

Will nodded. "What exactly do girls do in there? They always take forever!"

"When you're as ugly as Miranda, it takes a while to paint on your face," Mason replied with a snort.

Will sat up straight and gaped at me. "Is that the same Miranda from your photo?"

It seemed like I was going to need that mop after all. Will could barely keep his tongue in his mouth. "The very same."

Will pumped his fist. "Sweet!"

Mason gave him a sideways glance. "Why's that sweet?"

"Are you kidding me?" Will groaned as if he were eating a chocolate cake. "She's not ugly. She's smoking hot."

Mason gagged. "Only if you like hag."

"Bro, I know you're not into girls and shit, but damn. How can you say that? She's got a rocking body."

Mason held up one finger in warning. "If you don't stop, I'm gonna hurl all over you."

"Can you ever *not* be disgusting?"

The question brought our conversation to a stop. Miranda and Charlotte had returned. Their eyes rained a salvo of revulsion upon my grinning warlock. Why did he have to enjoy being himself so much?

Mason gave her the once-over before snorting. "I could ask you the same thing."

"We'd decided to help you." Miranda gazed down her nose at him. "I think I've changed my mind again."

"Don't get mad at them. It's my fault." Will's words drew everyone's shocked gazes. "I was the one being inappropriate."

Miranda arched one perfectly manicured eyebrow. "And just *who* are you?"

"I'm Will Hopkins." He stood and nodded to Miranda and Charlotte. "I just moved to Havenbridge."

A slight smile hitched up the corners of Miranda's lips. "*How* were you being inappropriate?"

Will's cheeks burned red. He tried to respond, but every time he opened his mouth, no sound came out. I had to hide my smile behind my hand to avoid cracking up. Straight guys weren't just weird, they were awful at flirting. "Well… I was saying… and I meant this as a compliment even though you might not think it is because… well—"

"Oh my God." Mason grabbed chunks of his hair and glanced up at the ceiling, apparently wishing to be struck dead by lightning. "Will you just tell her you think she has a 'rocking body' already?"

Will's gaze fell to the floor, his face redder than a baboon's butt.

"I see." Miranda tucked a chestnut strand of hair behind her ear, exposing her thin, white neck, and smiled. "Care to buy me a coffee, Will Hopkins?"

Her question pulled Will's gaze from the floor to Miranda. "Really?"

She placed her hand in his arm. "There's one thing you should know about me. I *never* say anything I don't mean." She then led him toward the counter.

"I think I'm gonna be sick." Mason dry-heaved like a cat trying to bring up a fur ball.

Charlotte smacked him upside the head and sat down at the table. "Be nice."

"Hey! When did you get so violent?" Mason rubbed the back of his head. "You used to be the nice sister."

"I still am, but being nice doesn't mean I let you be mean to *my* sister." She cocked an eyebrow at Mason, as if challenging him to utter one more negative comment about Miranda. I was impressed. Charlotte typically shied away from confrontation, preferring to be the peacemaker. Evidently that had changed.

Mason held up his hands in surrender. "Okay. Fine. I'll stop."

His quick submission caused Charlotte to part her lips in her usual angelic grin. "Good. So while my sister occupies your friend, why don't we get down to business?"

SHORTLY AFTER, Charlotte went over to her sister and asked her to keep Will distracted until we were done talking. Miranda didn't need to be asked twice. She let Will escort her to a far table, where they quietly chatted and laughed. It was nice to see Miranda on the receiving end of attention from a boy she liked. Most guys at our school were too intimidated by her intellect and gruff personality to approach her, much less admit they found her smoking hot.

"How much longer are you gonna play Peeping Tom?" Mason's question pulled my focus back to the table.

"Sorry. I'm just really happy for Miranda."

Charlotte glanced over at her sister and beamed. "Me too."

"The only thing I feel is sorry for Will." Mason's smirk turned into a grimace of pain when Charlotte popped him on the shoulder. "Hey! That hurt."

"Good," she chirped.

Why was I constantly cast as the referee? "Okay. Let's focus. We don't have a lot of time before we have to get goin'. We still have those ingredients to collect for Thad before we have to head home."

That comment got Charlotte's attention. "What spell is Thad attempting to cast?"

"Nuh-uh." Mason wagged his finger. "Ladies first."

She rolled her eyes. "Fine, but I better not get in trouble for this." I hoped she didn't either. She was taking a big risk by breaking protocol, but the information we shared could prove valuable to everyone. "A week ago the Conclave's magical alarms went off, and they asked my coven to look into it."

Mason's eyes met mine. The last time this happened, Ben Crane and his vampyre crony had flown into town and started killing people. That was how this whole mess got started. "A magical disturbance?"

"Well—" Charlotte grimaced and slightly shook her head. "They couldn't tell."

"What?" My question came out louder than I expected. Several customers looked over at me; even Will and Miranda had taken a break from their flirting to glance our way. I took a deep breath and tried again. "How is that possible?"

"They aren't sure, and neither are we," she answered with a shrug. "All they told us was that something foreign blipped on their radar, but ever since that first warning, they've sensed nothing."

"Like the spell Ben cast creating a magical blind spot around Havenbridge?" Mason asked.

Charlotte shook her head. "No. It was nothing like what happened during Mabon. They likened it to a missile being launched from a silo but then disappearing over the skies of Havenbridge."

That was a terrifying analogy. What had been fired at us, and where was it now? "And this couldn't be Icarian somehow arrivin' in town?"

Mason was the first to answer. "No. From what we've gathered about Icarian, he's extremely powerful. Someone like that would leave a magical wake wherever he went."

Charlotte nodded. "Which explains why he used Ben and Sersie to do his dirty work. They could slip in and out of town without sending up any red flags."

"What about the dark fae?" I asked. They were beings made entirely of magic and had been in league with Ben.

"No." Charlotte's tone was firm. "It's not something we've faced before. We've tried every incantation we could think of to reveal if this was any of our known enemies. This is an entirely new threat."

So a new foe *had* entered the stage, one that could fly under the Conclave's magical radar. Perhaps one of the reasons it was able to do that was because this being, for lack of a better word, hadn't entered town physically but arrived via my subconscious. "Tell us what you know about dreams."

Charlotte flinched slightly. "Dreams? What do they have to do with this?"

I glanced over at Mason, whose nod told me it was time for me to reveal why we were here. After I filled her in on my nightmares and the story behind my run-in with Aunt Millie, she clasped her hands on the table and stared silently into space. "So you think these dreams are some type of attack that are linked to your aunt Millie's warning?"

It certainly made sense. It was an obvious attempt to weaken us from the inside. "What else could it be?"

She glanced at Mason and then me. "Well, besides the obvious?"

"It's *not* an omen." Mason grabbed my hand and held it tight. "We've already dismissed that idea. It has to be something else."

After a few seconds, she nodded. "You're right. I'm sorry. You two love each other. There's no way that dream could ever come true, especially since you're spell bound."

Mason's sniff seemed to say *damn straight.*

"So then what could it be?"

Charlotte didn't have an immediate answer. She chewed on her bottom lip for several moments. "I really don't know. Most of what I know about dreams is that they sometimes foretell the future." Mason's scowl caused her to roll her eyes. "Which isn't the case here. I know. I'll have to check our Book of Shadows and see if I can find anything about dream magic in there."

The light smile that started on Mason's lips quickly grew warm and big. "Would you really do that for us?"

Charlotte beamed back. "Of course. We *are* friends, despite what you might think of us after everything."

Mason covered her hand with his. "I know."

"I have a question for you now." Charlotte locked eyes with Mason, evidently ready to determine if his answer would be as truthful as hers had been. "If you're coming to me for help, that tells me you don't have access to your Grimoire. That means your family is using your book of spells and you don't want to tip them off as to what you're up to. Why is that? What's going on?"

I expected Mason to either hem and haw or completely bend the truth. I was surprised when he disclosed Mr. Blackmoor's plan. Revealing the information was extremely risky. If Charlotte divulged any of it to her parents, we'd have the Conclave and the protector covens breaking down the front door to stop us.

When Mason finished, she sat back and rubbed her temples. "This is suicide, going up against Icarian without the other protector covens. Do you realize that?"

"Maybe," Mason answered. "But it's no different than when we faced Ben, the vampyren, and the dark fae all by ourselves in Otherworld. The Conclave didn't allow any of you to come with us. They practically sent us to our deaths."

Charlotte's scrunched lips revealed she couldn't argue that point.

"We survived that. We'll survive this."

"But this is an entirely different situation." Charlotte's eyes grew big and pleading as she clutched our hands. "Icarian is far more powerful than all our previous foes combined. You'll need us."

I squeezed her hand. "That's why we're here."

"Drake's right," Mason said. "We need you as much as you need us. Whether the Conclave or anyone wants to admit it or not, my family has been crucial in throwing wrenches into Icarian's plan from day one. There's got to be a reason for that. If you tell—"

"Okay. I won't." Her nod revealed she understood the consequences. "At least not now. But if you get in over your heads, I will. I'd rather your entire coven have its powers bound than die."

Mason's scowl told us he didn't like the sound of either, but what choice did we have? Charlotte was willing to help us and keep our plans a secret from her parents. This was the only way we could get to the bottom of my nightmares before whatever was responsible for them made its move.

CHAPTER 9

AFTER CHARLOTTE promised to get back to us as soon as she consulted her Book of Shadows, we had to practically take a crowbar to Will and Miranda to pry them apart. Their first meeting went so well that they made a date for next weekend before we dragged Will into Mason's car. Before we could collect the ingredients Thad needed for his spell, we had to take Will home.

All he had to do was survive the trip, and judging by how tightly Mason gripped the steering wheel as Will droned on and on about Miranda, the chances of that seemed pretty slim.

"So where to?" Mason's question interrupted Will's commentary on Miranda's assets.

"Just keep heading down Pleasant Street. I'll tell you where to turn." After answering the question, Will resumed the already five-minute monologue on her lips. It was getting to be a bit much.

"I'm glad you two hit it off."

"Hit it off?" Will repeated my words as if I'd uttered the single stupidest remark ever. "Hell yeah. She's got spunk, and I like that. She called me on all my bullshit. No other girl's ever done that before." His blue eyes nearly turned into pulsing cartoon hearts.

"You really want me to barf, don't you?"

Will chuckled at Mason's comment and sat so far forward in his seat that he might as well have climbed into the front with us. "Okay. Point taken. I'll shut up about her now."

Mason glanced over his shoulder at Will and pumped his fist. "Sweet!"

That brought all of us to laughter.

Will launched into a monologue about his father and how annoying his job was. Apparently Mr. Hopkins was an art collector or something. The details were a bit sketchy, but Will revealed his dad had worked for the Vatican and the Louvre. When he finally paused to take a breath, he pointed to the left. "Turn there."

When Mason made a left on Bessom Street, I winced. This was one of the ways he used to drive me home to Aunt Millie's.

"Can I ask you guys a question?"

I turned in my seat to face him. "Of course." I'd endure anything, even another lecture on how tasty Miranda's lips were, to avoid my thinking about my last visit to Aunt Millie's.

"Have you ever felt instantly connected to someone?"

I smiled over at Mason, who reached out to hold my hand.

"Yes," we both answered.

He sat back and sighed. "I mean it's crazy, but it's like something within me is telling me I'm supposed to meet Miranda. That's kind of how I felt when I met you, Drake. Like it was meant to be."

Mason glared over his shoulder. "What the hell does that mean?"

"Calm down." Will waved his hands like a white flag. "I'm not lusting after your boyfriend or anything. Is he a handsome guy? Sure. I'm man enough to admit when I find another dude attractive. But I'm straight."

"Then what are you talkin' about?" I asked.

Will studied the road outside his window for a few moments. A shadow fell over his previously carefree demeanor, and worry lines etched across his face. It was like he'd become someone else, or maybe this was who he really was underneath the bravado. "I just meant that I felt a kind of bond with Drake from the moment I saw him. I can't explain it other than to say it's nothing romantic. It was just like we were kindred spirits or something, and it was nice to feel that again, you know?"

I had an inkling, but I wasn't quite sure if I was right. "You've been alone for quite some time, huh?"

He nodded. "Ever since my mom passed away. My dad tries, but his idea of male bonding is riding my ass for shit he thinks I do wrong. So yeah, it's been pretty lonely. It doesn't help that every time I transfer to a new school, someone thinks they can kick me around for a few laughs."

Mason winced at that comment, and judging from his scrunched lips, he was regretting how he first treated Will. "I'm sorry about your mom. Drake and I have been there."

He glanced back and forth between us. "No shit?"

I shook my head.

"Well, I'm sorry too. It fucking sucks."

I definitely wouldn't argue with that.

Will sat forward again, this time pointing out the windshield. "You'll make a right up ahead on Anderson."

I tensed before shifting my gaze to Mason, who no longer focused on the road.

"What's the matter? You two look like you've seen a ghost."

I slowly returned my wide-eyed gaze to Will as Mason made the turn onto Anderson Street. "What's your address?"

"Eighty-seven Anderson Street. Why?"

Mason slammed on the brakes. A raging inferno blazed in his eyes. "You better tell me who the hell you are right the fuck now."

Instead of waiting for an answer, I got out of the car and slammed the door, hard. The white plumes of condensation that exited my mouth in short, rapid spurts told me it was cold, but I couldn't feel the sharp sting of the chilly air. My body had turned into a furnace, and I had to fight the urge to run.

Mason flew out of the car and wrapped me in his arms, his kisses and his touch telling me everything would be okay. That he would take care of everything.

Will exited the vehicle a second later. His eyes were wide as he approached us. "What the hell? Why the fuck are you so pissed off at me right now?"

Something was going on here. There was no way on God's green earth that Will happened to befriend me and move into my aunt Millie's house. This was no coincidence. This had the stench of magic all over it. I balled my fists at my sides, ready to defend myself or attack. "Who are you and what do you want from me?"

He stopped six feet from us and dropped his gaze to my fists. "Are you planning on trying to kick my ass?"

I didn't respond. I locked on to Will's cornflower blue eyes that had made me trust him the moment I laid eyes on him. Now, even the familiar eye color somehow seemed a part of a grand scheme. What kind of magic was this, and how the hell had Will managed to fool Mason's paranormal senses into thinking Will was human? "I'll do more than that if you don't tell me what it is you're after."

Will ran his fingers through his long blond hair and squinted. "I have no fucking clue what's going on right now. One moment we're laughing like fools and the next you're both going all batshit crazy on me. I think I should just get the fuck inside."

"Is that the way you want to play it?" Mason took several steps forward until he stood nose to nose with Will.

Although Will tensed, he didn't back up or avert his eyes. He locked gazes with Mason and held his ground. "I'm not playing a damn thing."

I couldn't take it anymore. I marched right up to him and crowded his space. "Right. You expect me to believe befriendin' me wasn't a part of some plan?"

"Part of what plan? What could I possibly gain by trying to be someone's friend?"

A whole hell of a lot. Ben had pretended to be a friend of the Blackmoors and even tried to seduce Thad for the sole purpose of killing us all. We'd let our guard down then, and we almost lost everything. "You tell me. Why are you pretendin' to want to be my friend, and why are you tryin' to weasel your way into my life?"

Will's eyes turned the same steely blue mine always did whenever I was cheesed off. "I'm not pretending jack shit, and I'm sure as fuck not trying to weasel my way into your life." He darted his gaze between us before stepping back and walking away. "Fuck the both of you."

I laughed, but there was no joy in the harsh sound that escaped my lips. "So you just happened to buy my aunt Millie's house? The house I used to live in and the one where she had her throat slashed open? Are you tellin' me this is just one happy coincidence?"

Will stopped and glanced back at me. "You used to live in my house?"

Mason snorted. "Don't pretend like you didn't already know that."

"I didn't. I swear." He held his hands in front of him. "I did know that someone had been ki—that something bad had happened here, but I had no idea it had been your aunt." He sighed and shoved his hands into the pockets of his jeans. "I'm sorry, bro. I truly am."

The piss and vinegar that roared through my blood slowly ebbed at the sincerity of Will's words. My soul and my heart overrode my brain and begged for me to trust him. It was like he and I were somehow meant to be. In fact, it reminded me of Mason, but in a different way.

When I met Mason, it was like I was suddenly orbiting the sun. That was how powerful the force that drew me to him was. With Will, it was more like he was the moon that had always been orbiting around me, which didn't make a hill of beans worth of sense. Still, the pull he somehow had on my soul proved too hard to fight. I unclenched my fists and sighed. "You really had no idea?"

"None." He shook his head once and met my gaze. "I swear."

And I believed him. "Okay."

"What?" Mason gaped at me. "Are you serious?"

"He's tellin' the truth. I can feel it."

A smile spread across Will's lips. "Really?"

Mason gripped my hand. It was his way of asking if I was certain.

I gave him a nod and my answer. "Really." Even though Mason wasn't entirely convinced, judging by the way he eyed Will, he trusted my intuition enough to release his anger with one long exhalation.

"Thank God." Will walked back toward us. "Now would you mind telling me why you freaked out like that? Are you two bipolar or something?"

"That's not very PC, you know?"

"And you're not answering my question," he said with a poke to my shoulder.

I eyed him before turning my attention to Aunt Millie's house. "I'm not bipolar. Just cautious."

"No shit. You practically accused me of stalking you." He turned around and stared at the house with us. "But why?"

How was I going to explain my reaction without telling him about magic and vampyren and warlocks and shadow weavers? "I've just been through a lot in the past year."

"Like what?"

I blew all the air from my lungs. "You don't want to hear my shit."

"Sure I do." He knocked into my shoulder with his. "That's what friends do, right?"

It was, but I couldn't tell him the truth. If I did, the Conclave would order Will's memories wiped just like they tried, and failed, to do to me. There was no way I was going to subject Will to that.

"Come on. Tell me." His warm smile made me forget I was standing outside in the cold.

"Before my aunt died, I lost my parents in a car accident." My chest tightened as it did whenever I talked about their deaths.

Will's smile retreated. "Fuck! You've had it rough. Your parents and aunt in one year?"

I nodded. "Thankfully the Blackmoors took me in."

Will's eyes drew into big circles. "You didn't have anyone else? Any other family you could have lived with?"

I shook my head in response. My last family member was the woman who had begged me to kill her inside this house a few days ago.

Mason pulled me against him, and I melted at his touch. "I'm his family now."

Will stood in stunned silence for a moment, evidently trying to digest the disaster that was my life.

"Hey, boys!" Mr. Hopkins stood at the open front door, and I cringed. Aunt Millie used to greet Mason and me the exact same way whenever he brought me home. "I've made some hot chocolate. Come on in and have some."

"They can't, Dad," Will yelled to his father. "They've got things to do."

Mr. Hopkins waved his son's words away. "Nonsense. There's always time for hot chocolate on a cold day." He descended the porch steps and gestured for us. "I won't take no for an answer."

Before Will could start what would likely be an argument, I grabbed his forearm and shook my head. "It's fine."

"What?" Mason turned me around in his arms, his eyebrows drawn close together. "You don't have to do this."

"Mason's right," Will said. "I'll deal with my dad. You two just go."

I shook my head. For reasons I couldn't explain, I had to go in there.

As soon as I entered the house, the heavenly smell of hot chocolate brought me right back to my first night here. I'd been settling in my room and doing an awful lot of crying when the creamy, sweet scent of cocoa filled the air with the rich warmth of home. I sucked back my tears and followed the aromatic trail to Aunt Millie at the kitchen table. We sat and talked for hours about my parents as we drank cup after cup of her special brew.

It had been the first time I'd been able to discuss my parents without breaking down, but it was something I needed to do. I had to remember the good times we shared and not the unexplained tragedy of their deaths. Aunt Millie had known that, and it was the first of many wonderful things she'd done for me.

"Are you okay?" Mason sat next to me on the black leather couch that seemed out of place in Aunt Millie's living room.

I took his hand in mine and trailed my touch along his thin fingers. His familiar flesh kept me anchored. "I will be."

Mason peered into the kitchen, where Will had escorted his dad shortly after we entered the house. The whispered voices told me exactly what they were talking about. "I don't understand why you agreed to come back in here. Why do that to yourself?"

I shrugged. I couldn't explain it. Maybe it was to say one final good-bye since the last one didn't go as planned. Maybe it was to prove I could be in this house and not have something awful happen to me. Or maybe it was just to see how much the house had changed, and boy had it ever. Cold leather furniture, masculine woods, and an unusual scent I recognized but couldn't identify had replaced Aunt Millie's soft, feminine style.

Whatever the reason, my desire to enter this house one final time had pulled on my gut like a magnet. I was supposed to be here.

Mr. Hopkins reentered the room, carrying a tray with four black mugs of cocoa. "Drake. Mason." His words were soft and gentle, a definite departure from his usual abrasiveness. "I must apologize for… forcing you to come inside. I didn't realize—"

"It's fine. You didn't know." I took one of the cups from the tray. My trembling hand upset the liquid, which splashed over the rim and onto my jeans. Mason immediately grabbed a napkin and blotted me. "I'm the one who should be sorry for bein' so clumsy."

Mr. Hopkins took a cup for himself and sat in his leather wingback chair. "No need to apologize. I've lived with Will for eighteen years. I'm used to cleaning up messes."

"Thanks, Dad." Will snagged a cup and sat next to Mason and me on the couch.

"You boys don't have to be polite and stay." Mr. Hopkins took a sip from his cup and settled his crisp gaze on me. "I just wanted to say thank you for allowing my son to hang out with you today, and I thought hot chocolate would do the trick."

Mason flashed that fake smile of his and took the last mug. "It's very thoughtful. Thank you."

"What was thoughtful was you coming inside to appease me after what happened here." He pressed his rough lips into a thin line. "I don't think I could have done that."

Mason cocked his head to one side and regarded our host. An unusual expression crashed upon his features. It appeared to be a cross between a curious cat and an alert guard dog. "But you can buy a house knowing it was the scene of an unsolved murder?"

"That's a good question." Mr. Hopkins cradled his cup in his lap and sat back. "I've always been attracted to locales or objects with a history of danger. It's why I joined the Marines and fought in the Middle East. It's also why I work for the Orion Group."

I glanced at Will, who seemed to have checked out of the conversation, and back to his father. "But I thought you worked in art. At least that's what Will told us."

The mention of his name got Will's attention. "Wait. What did I say?" After Mason repeated what I'd said, he turned to his father. "But that is what you do. Right?"

Mr. Hopkins offered a single nod in reply.

Unless he was involved in illegal activities, his answer made no sense. "Art isn't a job usually associated with danger, is it?"

"Not usually, no," Mr. Hopkins answered. "But the Orion Group is a privately run organization that procures priceless artifacts for an exclusive clientele."

Yeah, that didn't sound legit at all.

Mason emptied half his cup, ready to finish the drink and get out of here. "And that's dangerous how?"

"Well, most of the pieces our clients are interested in buying are not easily found and are usually one of a kind. For example, Picasso's *The Painter* was thought to be lost in a plane crash in Nova Scotia before pieces of it were 'recovered.' While the painting had been aboard the aircraft, the complete work, not the forgery, had actually made its way into Saudi Arabia, where I tracked it to the home of Amina Nassar, a despicable individual living in the Al Jouf province."

"Holy shit!" Will sat forward so quickly he almost dropped his full cup of hot chocolate. "So you what? Stole it from him?"

"Not at all. I retrieved it," Mr. Hopkins answered with a click of his tongue. "In fact, he downed the plane just to get his hands on the painting. I merely took what wasn't his. I've done the same in India, Papua New Guinea, sub-Saharan Africa, and most recently Europe."

His nonchalant attitude toward his adventures worried me but not Will. His estimation of his brusque father had just doubled, if Will's wide-open mouth was any indication. I wasn't sold that his actions were anything to be impressed by. "So you steal art from art thieves?"

Mr. Hopkins chuckled. "An art thief might look at it that way, but I don't. I see it as rescuing the art from undesirables and placing it in the hands of a more suitable owner."

Suddenly I remembered one of the things Will told us earlier about where his father had previously worked. "Like the Louvre or the Vatican?"

In reply, he raised an eyebrow and glanced at his son. "I see Will has been quite talkative."

Will shrugged. "When people ask questions, I tend to give them answers."

And that seemed to be a big difference between Will and his father. Will answered questions as honestly as he could. In fact, he often told you more than you really wanted to know. His rambling about Miranda was a case in point. His father's responses were different, almost rehearsed, but I wasn't going to admit that out loud.

What I needed to do was follow Mason's lead and finish my drink so we could leave. I brought the cup to my lips and sipped. Mr. Hopkins definitely didn't make it like Aunt Millie did. His hot chocolate had a weird kind of sweetness. It reminded me of parsnip, and I quickly put it back on the tray.

"Not a fan of my hot chocolate?" Mr. Hopkins gazed at me over the rim of his cup.

"It's wonderful," I lied. "I'm just full from my drink at Starbucks."

He nodded as if he understood. "Well, you tried it. That's all that matters. But I fear my frankness with you about my job has sullied your perception of me. I assure you the Orion Group operates within international law. Otherwise, instead of being here, I'd be in jail."

His comment raised a question I hadn't thought of before. "Is that why you're here in Havenbridge? To collect a lost, priceless piece of art?"

"You're very perceptive." He winked at me before setting his cup on the table next to mine. "I am here to collect an extremely rare object. I just have to find it first, but I have a pretty good lead."

"What is it?" If Will were standing, he'd be jumping up and down. "Maybe I could help."

His father arched a blond eyebrow at him. "Really? This is the first time you've shown real interest in my work."

"This is the first time I've found your work interesting," Will admitted with a snort.

Mr. Hopkins laughed, but there was no joy in the sound or glint in his eye. "Maybe I'll tell you later. I'm sure Mason and Drake have more important things to do than listen to me talk about my job."

"Although it has been… enlightening"—Mason stood and fished his keys out of his pocket—"Drake and I have several stops to make before heading home."

"Of course." Mr. Hopkins rose and offered his hand to Mason. "Thanks again for being kind to my son."

Mason shook it before glancing back at Will. "I'd say it was no problem, but he can be a real pain in the ass."

Will flipped him off.

Mr. Hopkins laughed. "Tell me about it."

While the three of them bantered like fraternity brothers, I collected the dishes and placed them on the tray.

"That isn't necessary." Mr. Hopkins moved to take them from my hand.

I went the opposite way around the living room to avoid his reach. "It's the least I could do for your hospitality."

After he smiled and nodded in approval, I headed toward the entrance to the kitchen, which was located to the right of a large curio cabinet containing knickknacks and photos. I paused before it, glancing at the pictures of Will as a young boy, proudly displayed on the glass shelves. The majority of them were generic school photos kids posed for each year with a photographer who never really cared if he got the best shot. None of the pictures of Will featured him and his parents around the house, on vacation, or opening presents on Christmas.

That was a little bizarre. My parents had had tons of candid photos of me all over the house. Heck, even Aunt Millie had some from our brief time together. Maybe the Hopkinses weren't picture people. As I was about to continue on, a photo on the fourth shelf caught my eye.

A cobalt-blue house with white shutters and a wraparound porch sat in a valley of green. Behind it towered a large white mountain. I dropped the tray and an explosion of shattering dishes filled the silence that had engulfed the room. Mason stood at my side, clutching at my shoulders, trying to get me to look at him, but all I could focus on was the picture of the house from my dreams—except in the photo, it wasn't abandoned and falling apart.

Suddenly everything went black.

CHAPTER 10

As I ran through a pitch-black room, trying to find a place to hide, my world spun. I was moments away from passing out. If I did, I'd be dead.

But why?

Needles of searing pain tore through my stomach as a not-so-gentle reminder that I'd been seriously wounded. My plaid shirt had been turned into a shredded rag, and blood freely poured from an open wound on my side.

The memory of Mason standing over me and trying to kill me flooded back to my consciousness.

I held my breath. I was back in my dream. How was that possible, and how the heck was I still alive? The last time I was here, Mason fired at me point-blank.

A loud hum filled the air. As if I were on a free-running course, I dove through a doorway and rolled into the hall. The wall to my right exploded in a cloud of plaster and debris. The Mason from my nightmare obviously still wanted me dead, and if I didn't find shelter, he was going to get his wish.

A few feet ahead of me stood a wooden staircase. I jumped to my feet and sprinted up the steps. Another explosion turned the banister where my hand had just been into splinters. The force propelled me forward, but I caught the wall with my left foot, kicked off, and landed back on the stairs in one leap.

"Just give up already." Mason's English-accented voice drifted up the staircase as I made it to the second story. "You have no weapons and nowhere to go. Well, except to hell, where you belong."

Three open doorways lined the hall upstairs, and I darted into the farthest one and shut the door, not that it would do much good. Mason's magic would make short work of the temporary barrier, but with luck, it would buy me a few seconds to find something to defend myself with or at the very least figure out what the hell was going on.

I sprinted for the closet, tossing out boxes and clothes in my vain search for a weapon, but this wasn't where the remaining arsenal was stored. Those weapons were located in the basement or in the downstairs closet.

I paused. How the heck did I know that?

A light rap on the door got my attention.

"We both know you're in there, and we both know you won't find anything useful in that room."

"You're awfully confident for a solitary warlock with no coven and mediocre powers." Why the hell did I say that, and what happened to the Southern drawl Mason always teased me about?

"Is that what you're going to use against me? Insults?" Mason snorted. "What happened to the wit I used to love?"

Used to love? "Why are you doing this? Why are you trying to kill me? We love each other."

"Are you daft?" Venom dripped from his words. "You betrayed me. You made a bloke like me believe he had actually found something to live for, something that would always be mine, but none of it was ever real. You lied to me about what you truly were."

I had no clue what Mason was going on about, but I used the distraction to search the rest of the closet and the chest of drawers, only to come up empty. That was when I remembered the hemlock we kept stashed in the nightstand along with a spare pistol, just in case one of these monsters broke in during the night.

Wait a minute. Mason wasn't a monster. He was the boy I loved. And hemlock? Why did "we" keep a poisonous weed around?

"Why did you have to lie?" Mason roared in fury as he punched and kicked the door.

If Mason really wanted in here, the door would be exploding inward and I'd be gazing at the wrong side of one of his power blasts. He was stalling.

I sprinted to the nightstand. Inside the top drawer sat another pistol with the butt of the gun shaped into a dragon's claw, just like the one I had held downstairs. A small plastic bag containing a brown powder peeked out underneath the barrel.

"Answer me!" The anger in his inflection wavered, replaced by the unmistakable notes of desperation mashed up with hesitancy. He didn't really want to kill me. Yes, he was livid, but only because of whatever betrayal he believed I was guilty of. Deep down, he still loved me. I could feel it, and I could use that to my advantage.

"I never lied to you." I emptied the bullets from the cylinder and popped them in my mouth, wincing at the bitter metallic tang, while I opened the bag. While my mind had no clue what I was doing, my body sure seemed to have a plan. I spat out the saliva-coated bullets. After placing them in the bag, I gave it a good shake until they were covered with the powder.

"So you did love me?" The hope in his voice told me he truly wanted to cling to those words more than anything in the world. What did he think I had done?

I shoved the ammunition back into the cylinder and closed it. I let out a deep breath as I faced the door and held the weapon safely behind my back. "I still do. With all my heart. You have to know that, Mason."

The door exploded inward, and I shielded my eyes from the spraying needles of wood. He stepped over the debris, his gorgeous blue eyes aflame with murder and his hands glowing with scarlet energy. "You continue to lie."

I took a step back, eyeing all possible avenues as I typically did while parkouring, until the barrel of the gun scraped the wall behind me. "I'm not lying."

"Is that why you've called me by some other man's name twice in one evening?"

Now this made some sort of sense. Whatever magic had pulled Mason and me into this nightmare had somehow altered his memories. All I had to do was get him to remember me, to remember us. "Your name *is* Mason. Mason Blackmoor. You come from a powerful coven, and your family has served as the protector coven for the Order of Black for four generations."

He cocked his head to one side. "You *are* daft."

"No, I'm not." I took one tentative step forward. "Mason, please…."

After mumbling a word in Latin, Mason suddenly held me pinned to the wall by my neck. "Don't call me that name ever again." He balled his free hand into a fist, sending spindles of red energy arcing into the air. "I don't know what kind of game you're playing now, but I want to hear you say my name before I end this once and for all."

I had no clue what he wanted me to say, so all I could do was struggle against his grip. If I could get free, my gifted speed and dexterity would give me the chance I needed, but whatever incantation he'd spoken made that impossible. His grip had turned to steel, and if I didn't find a way to free myself, he was going to kill me. My only way out of this seemed to be the pistol I still held behind my back, but I couldn't do it. No matter what magic had corrupted his memories, he was still the boy I loved, the one who made me feel safe, the one who covered my heart with kisses and my soul with love.

I was *not* going to kill him.

"Say it!" Red sparks shot out of his hands like meteors, as if the angrier he got, the more powerful he became. "Now!"

He eased up the pressure on my neck just long enough for me to utter a name I'd never heard in my life. "Finlay Appleton."

As if I'd uttered my own spell, something unlocked within me. My mind and the body that had been moving me around my dream merged into one. My eyes drew into slits, and a hatred I had never felt before consumed me from within. I brought the pistol forward and shoved it into his chest, right above his heart.

Finlay glanced down at it, his eyes wide, and the hatred within bled into pure fear.

I pulled the trigger. A clap of thunder filled the room as he released his grip on my neck. I fired again. A bloom of red spread across his shirt as he staggered backward, glancing between the fatal wound and me. Tears fell from his eyes, and a second later a stream of red energy fired from his hands, striking me in the chest.

The force of the blast sent me barreling into the wall and Finlay tumbling to the ground. A huge hole filled with jagged bone and gore took up residence where my chest had been.

"Are you happy?" He managed to prop himself against the dresser, struggling for breath and attempting to use his magic to heal his wounds. That wasn't going to happen, and he realized that. The hemlock was working its way into his system, preventing him from accessing his perverted abilities. The effect was only temporary, but it would last long enough to do the job. "Now we both die."

"Yes." My breath became shallow, and a numbing chill spread like a glacier across my flesh. "It's how this was always meant to end."

I WOKE up clawing at the dry, cold earth underneath me. Frantically, I scoured my surroundings, expecting to see Finlay/Mason lying in a pool of blood. Only darkness deeper than the shadows Mason commanded greeted me.

When I tried to sit up, sharp pains shot through my head and stars rocketed across my vision. One sweep of my hand along the back of my head revealed a nasty goose egg. How the heck had that happened? I hadn't suffered a head wound. I'd been shot in the—

My hand flew to my chest. Instead of a gaping hole, I found only my sweater, which was sopping wet. In fact, every square inch of me was moist, most likely from the night sweats that had accompanied my dream. My damp skin, combined with the cool air, made me shiver. Who the heck had opened a window in the middle of a New England winter?

"Mason?" My voice came out in a rasp, as if I'd been struggling for breath for hours. I cleared my throat and tried again. "Is anyone there?"

I listened for a reply but received none.

I tried to force myself off the ground, but my legs wouldn't move and a fog seemed to have set up permanent residence in my brain. My throat burned, my muscles ached, and no matter how many times I swallowed, I couldn't stop my mouth from filling with saliva. Had I been drugged?

"Drake."

I recognized the voice even though I couldn't see him. I sat up slowly, taking care not to move too suddenly and pass out again. "Mr. Hopkins? Where am I? What happened?"

"Don't worry. You're safe."

"That's not what I asked you."

"What do you think happened?"

If I knew that, I sure as heck wouldn't be asking.

"Think about it. Tell me what you remember."

I shook my head, doing my best to force the nightmare from my mind, but I instantly regretted it. My vision swam and the rocketing stars returned, except this time they brought friends with them. I had to ease myself back onto the hard-packed earth. "I c-can't. It hurts."

"I'm sure it does." Why could I hear a smile in his voice? "But it's important that you remember."

"We were at Aunt Mill—your house, drinkin' hot chocolate and talkin'. But it was time to go, so Mason—" I sat up, and even though a thousand daggers stabbed at my brain, I peered into the darkness. "Where's Mason? Is he okay?"

"He's… fine. He wasn't feeling well, so Will took him to lie down."

I struggled to get up. "I want to see him."

"Not right now. Just lie back down."

"No." Even though my arms were weak and my legs trembled beneath me, I managed to get myself into a kneeling position. "I want to see him now."

"I said lie back down!" He barked the words like a drill sergeant who expected complete obedience at all times.

Unfortunately for him, I wasn't a part of his squad. I stood up on wobbly legs and glared into the darkness. "Take me to him or get the hell out of my way."

Applause reverberated in the darkness. "You've got balls, son. Not that I'm surprised, considering everything." The respect in his tone turned into a snarl. "But you'll sit your ass back down or I'll put a pistol to your boyfriend's brains and blow them the fuck out of his head."

My legs gave out and I crashed back onto the ground. Even though venom coursed through my body, I didn't give it voice. If I did, Mason was going to pay the price. "I don't understand what's goin' on."

I didn't like hearing the tremor in my voice, but Mr. Hopkins did. He chuckled because he believed my fear meant he had won. Little did he know he had already lost. It wouldn't be long before the Blackmoors started scrying for our location, and when they found us, they'd make him pay for whatever he'd done to me and to Mason.

"I know you don't understand."

Now that I'd grown accustomed to the dark, I detected his voice on my right. I concentrated in that direction as if I could magically make his form appear.

"That is why you must remember your dream."

My breath hitched. "How did you know about my dream?"

"I know a great many things, Drake. I'll share them all with you, but first you must remember your dream."

No. I didn't want to. It was too horrible, and just thinking about it not only made me shiver, it rattled the foundation of everything I held dear. "No. It's just a stupid dream. It means nothin'."

"It means *everything*. You have no idea how special you are, do you?" His gruff tone gave way to one of wonder and awe. "Within you lies so much untapped potential just waiting to be released, and it wants to be released. It *begs* to be released, and all you need is to use the key."

Flint Hopkins was mad. He was talking about me as if I were a magical being, some sprite with the power to level mountains and change the course of mighty rivers. I was nothing special. I was Drake Carpenter, the boy who had fallen in love with a warlock. Nothing more.

"You have to remember. You have to come back to us."

"Come back to you?"

"Back to *us*. Back to where you belong."

I was wrong. He wasn't mad. He was a stark raving lunatic. "I don't belong with you. I belong with Mason, with the Blackmoors. *They* are my family."

"That's where you're wrong."

Lights suddenly flooded the room, and I shielded my eyes from the glare. After I adjusted to the fluorescence, I found myself in a basement, but it wasn't the basement in Aunt Millie's house. Mr. Hopkins sat on a metal crate wearing a black combat suit. A dark blue logo decorated the upper right corner of his chest. Within the insignia was a white outline of a man holding a bow in the aiming position. The words *Orion Group* were written in white letters underneath the figure.

"And why's that?" I found the strength to sit up and meet his crisp gaze.

He held his arms open as if expecting an embrace. "Because *I* am your real family."

"You must think I'm stupid or incredibly naïve." I stood up and kept one eye on Mr. Hopkins while I did a quick survey of the basement. Metal crates lined the perimeter, and about twenty feet away, a staircase led up to the first floor. My mind quickly mapped out the best way to escape and evade Mr. Hopkins. Once full strength had returned to my legs, I would make a run for it, find Mason, and then get the hell out of here. "You are *not* my family."

A grin stretched wide across his features. "I know it's hard to believe. I had trouble believing it myself, but as soon as I heard about you, I came to Havenbridge to see if it was true. After I met you, I still wasn't certain, considering what you had aligned yourself with, but the pull was there. I felt it. Didn't you?"

The only thing I felt was pity for someone who had lost all shreds of his sanity.

"Oh, I know you probably didn't feel a connection with me. We hardly spent any time together, but Will was a different story, wasn't he? You bonded with him quickly, didn't you?"

My jaw tensed. I had felt close with Will almost from the moment I met him, and I hadn't understood why.

"The two of you spent a lot of time together when you were babies. Well, at least before those damn witches took you from your parents."

Witches? Did he know about magic, or was he using the word as slang? "My parents?"

"Yes, and I'm not talking about the Carpenters. Those hicks took you in after the witches kidnapped you and killed your *real* parents, your biological parents." He settled the full weight of his cornflower blue eyes on me, as if daring me to gaze deep into the crisp, clear pools. I did.

Blake and Drew Carpenter had brown eyes, and so did Aunt Millie, but Mr. Hopkins and Will had the same light blue hue I saw every time I gazed into a mirror.

No. It couldn't be. It had to be coincidence.

"I'm your uncle Flint."

FOR WHAT felt like an eternity, I stood there in silence, processing the madness my "uncle Flint" tried to get me to believe. My stomach revolted from the information, churning the words in my guts like acid. The logical part of my brain didn't believe it. It dismissed the information as lies sculpted by Icarian or some other supernatural foe. To what end, I wasn't certain, but they were designed to come between Mason and me.

But there was a part of me, a small part somewhere deep in my soul, that believed differently. That part of me clung to Flint's words as if they were a life preserver.

I wasn't going to let that part of me win. The Carpenters were my parents. End of discussion.

I held my chin high and leveled my gaze down upon my self-proclaimed uncle. "What's your angle?"

His eyes grew wide as if he were more innocent than a newborn babe. "You mean other than reclaiming a part of my family I'd believed to be lost forever?"

I crossed my arms over my chest. "You need to keep your stories straight. You can't say I was lost to you *and* claim to know what happened after I was kidnapped and given to a family of 'hicks,' as you said."

"Uncle" Flint leaned back and sighed. "I didn't find out about you or the Carpenters until recently. After you were kidnapped, we searched for you everywhere, and we even found the two witches who had taken you. No matter what we did to them—and believe me, we tried everything—those women wouldn't tell us where they stashed you or why."

"You tortured them?"

He snorted. "Of course. They were scum. When we realized they would rather die than tell us what they knew, we gave them what they wanted."

I gulped. "You killed them." His nod almost made me vomit. "If I had been truly kidnapped, why not call the cops? Why not post my picture everywhere?"

"And let the world know that a Hopkins had been taken?" He shook his head as if I couldn't do basic arithmetic. "You wouldn't be alive today if we had done that. The safest thing for you was to keep looking, and we did. For years. But every lead ended in a dead end." He pushed off the crate and took several steps toward me. When he was within reaching distance, he attempted to place his hands on my shoulders, but I backed away. He nodded and took two steps back. "I never gave up. I knew one day I'd find you, and now, here we are."

"Yet you said you didn't believe I was your nephew at first. Now you suddenly do. Why is that?"

"Well, your resemblance to my brother is uncanny. You look just like the boy I grew up with, but I couldn't base my decision on your appearance. I needed more, which was why I urged Will to develop a relationship with you."

I tensed. "Will knew?"

A loud burst of laughter told me he didn't. "Are you kidding me? I love my son, but he isn't the sharpest tool in the shed. He's been a disappointment to me, and his lack of interest in the family business has been an unusual anomaly."

"Family business?"

He pointed to the insignia on his outfit. "The Orion Group. I don't work for the company. I *am* the company. It's been our family's legacy for countless generations, and I'd hoped it'd be Will's one day. Sadly, I don't think that will happen. He doesn't have your strength of character or fierce determination. He's weak. Just like his mother was."

There was no way I could be related to someone so cruel or callous. If by some twist of fate I was, then I owed a huge debt of gratitude to those women who plucked me from that family and placed me in a nurturing and loving home.

"So bein' nice to your son is what convinced you we were related?"

He gave me a wink and a smile. "It certainly helped. Like I said, you and Will had been real close, but that wasn't what convinced me. The hot chocolate did the trick."

"The hot chocolate?" I arched an eyebrow. Flint got crazier by the minute.

"Not the hot chocolate itself. But what was *in* it."

So I *had* been drugged. "You poisoned me?"

He laughed. "Well, I suppose that would be true had you not been my nephew, but fortunately for you, our family has developed an immunity to hemlock."

My mind reeled. Not only had I dreamed about using hemlock, but it was extremely toxic to everyone. How the heck was any of this even possible?

"But the real clincher was your reaction to the house."

I'd almost forgotten about the photo. It was the last thing I had seen before I woke up in my dream, which took place inside that very house. "What makes that house so important?"

"It's been in our family for hundreds of years, and only the strongest, most powerful of us react to it as you did. *That* was when I knew without a doubt that you were my nephew, Matthew Hopkins."

Hearing the name sent me spinning on a Tilt-A-Whirl, and I stumbled backward.

Flint suddenly stood by my side, grasping my shoulders. His eyes were wide and a huge smile stretched across his big, mean face. "You remember, don't you?"

I couldn't answer. Something deep within me awoke and swam to the surface of my consciousness. It kicked wildly in a frantic rush to be free, but I took a deep breath, imagining an anchor weighing it down. Whatever fought its way to the surface once again sank beneath the waters.

I shrugged out of his touch and stepped back. "Why should I believe one word that comes out of your mouth? If I am your nephew, then why are you holdin' me hostage and keepin' me from my boyfriend?"

"Let's not ruin this reunion by talking about Mason." His upper lip curled into a sneer.

"What do you have against him? You should be grateful to Mason and his family for takin' me in and watchin' over me since Aunt Millie died."

He tsked. "She's *not* your aunt. Sh—"

"Millicent Carpenter *is* my aunt." My tone was firm. This was not up for debate.

His deep breath communicated he realized that.

"So tell me. Why do you hate Mason so much?"

He scratched his fingers across his scalp and sighed. "You mean you haven't figured it out yet? Come on, Matthew. *Think!*"

I clenched my teeth. "My name is Drake."

"No. Your name is Matthew Hopkins. You were named after one of the most powerful and influential men in our history. You are the one we have waited for, the key to the victory for a war that has secretly been waged across this planet. You are the one who can finally help humans destroy the greatest threat to our existence—the *homo magus*."

I gasped. How did he know about the magical community? The only humans who knew of their existence were—

"Y-you're a witch hunter?"

He bared his full set of teeth. "Yes. And so are you."

CHAPTER 11

"Where are you takin' me?"

Flint didn't answer my question. Instead, he gestured at the four muscled meatheads dressed like commandos who had stormed down the basement stairs a few moments ago. They grabbed me by the arms and half dragged, half carried me up the steps and out to the main floor.

They brought me into what resembled a mess hall. Commercial ovens and cooking stations sat along the left wall. To the right, rows of tables filled the remainder of the room. Although the seats were empty, if they had been occupied, at least a hundred people could comfortably have enjoyed a meal in here.

"Where's Mason? I want to see him."

The goons on either side of me grunted in disapproval and increased their steely grips on my arms before hauling me outside.

The sun shone high in the sky, and a warm breeze gently kissed my face. How long had I been unconscious? It had been late afternoon and winter the last time I'd been outside. I couldn't be in Massachusetts anymore. I had to be somewhere down South or on the West Coast. "Where am I?"

The only answer I received was a sniff as I was rudely escorted onto what reminded me of a military base. Enormous Quonset-style structures flanked either side of the concrete walkway, but instead of wearing standard military uniforms, the people who marched about wore outfits similar to my chatty escorts' and Flint's. A barbed-wire fence encircled the compound for as far as I could see, and at regular intervals, watchtowers with armed guards high on their perches looked out over the grounds inside and outside of the enclosure.

After a ten-minute walk, we entered the largest structure on the right. Soldiers in black set up chairs around an enormous cage, at least fifty yards wide, which contained what reminded me of an indoor free-running course.

I had no clue what was going on, but I wasn't taking another step until someone gave me an answer. I put on the brakes, trying to force my way out of the grips of the men on either side of me. "Tell me what's goin' on. Right. Now."

Something hard jammed against my back. "Don't make me kill you."

I glanced over my shoulder at the twisted face of one of the guards from the basement. Flint stood behind him, his expression stony and unreadable. He wasn't coming to my defense. If I only had me to worry about, I'd tell him to just hurry up and get it over with, but I still had no clue what had become of Mason. I had to stay alive long enough to find out and get him out of here.

After taking several deep breaths, I allowed myself to be escorted toward the cage, where I was rudely shoved inside. Walls of various heights and slants spanned almost the entire length and width of the enclosed area. Ramps led up to platforms that either came to dead ends or were connected to the web of pipes constructed over the course. After a brief scan, I had several paths already mapped out, depending on what exactly I was facing.

The sound of the cage locking behind me drew my attention. The guard with the gun smirked before turning to Flint and nodding.

"Is this what happens at a typical Hopkins family reunion?"

He grinned. "No, but then you're not a typical member of the family, are you?"

He was right about that. I had a heart and a soul and wasn't a psychopath. "Would you mind tellin' me why I'm in this cage?"

"You're here to show us exactly what you can do."

I arched an eyebrow at him. "You want to watch me parkour?"

"No." He gripped the bars of the cage and pulled close. "I want to watch you be a witch hunter."

My mouth hung open as I heard the sound of another cage door opening and closing at the opposite end from where I stood. I spun around, but I couldn't see anyone. The walls inside the cage hid whatever was happening on the other end. "Are you serious?"

"Of course." Flint nodded to the soldiers who had gathered around him, and the majority of them took their seats. "I've heard tales about what you can do, but I want to see it for myself." Two men suddenly appeared at his side. One held a pistol with a dragon claw and the other a rapier. Flint took them and held them up to me. "These are the weapons of a true witch hunter. While many spend years learning how to use them to slay our enemies, only a choice few of us are born with the innate ability to wield them. As a descendent of Matthew Hopkins, you are one such individual." He placed his hands and the weapons through the opening between the bars and offered them to me.

I stepped back and shook my head. "I'm not playin' your perverted version of the Hunger Games."

"Suit yourself." He dropped them onto the floor in front of me. "From what I've heard, you may not even need them."

"What are you talkin' about?"

He shot me a blank stare, as if the answer was obvious. "Your immunity to magic. If it's true, you represent the beginning of a new breed of witch hunter even more unique than Matthew Hopkins, the first and only one of us to ever be able to detect and avoid magic. If you are immune to spells, then his gift has not only passed on to you but has grown into something we can use to eradicate every last one of the *homo magus*."

"I won't hurt anyone." I squared my shoulders and glared at him. "Especially not for you."

The grin that practically sawed his face in half told me he'd been expecting that answer. "How about for him?"

I followed his nod to the center of the cage, where Will stood between two armed guards. "Dad? Drake? What the fuck is going on?"

"Now you have to make a decision." He held up his hand, and in response, the floor in the center of the course opened up and a cage containing a young woman no older than me came into view. She'd been beaten. Angry cuts slashed across her cheek and chin. Her clothes had been mostly shredded, and she gripped the bars in a murderous rage. "Do nothing and let that witch kill you and Will, or save yourselves and kill the witch."

"How can you do this?" My words were barely a whisper. "He's your son."

"And he's *your* cousin. That's why I know you'll make the right decision."

The cage door opened and the woman sprinted out. The guards on either side of Will raised their weapons, but she mumbled a spell that sent the soldiers flying headfirst into the iron bars.

"Holy shit!" Will spun around and attempted to seek shelter behind one of the walls. Before he took two steps, she raised one hand and a stream of water flew out of her palm, striking Will in the back. He slammed hard into the wall, and though he did his best to deflect the water she aimed at his face, he couldn't defend against the constant barrage. She advanced on him, unleashing a steady stream in an effort to drown him.

I glanced at the weapons next to me. They called to something within me, a part of me that begged me to pick them up and put them to their righteous use. I turned my back on them and the seductive voice and bolted toward the witch. Even though she was scared and fighting for her life, I couldn't let her kill Will. I grabbed her shoulder and spun her around. "Stop it! He's not your enemy."

Her power shut off, and Will took several gasping breaths and coughed up a lungful of water.

The witch stepped back, an angry scowl on her face. "But you are, aren't you, witch hunter?" She circled around me like a hyena waiting to take down her prey while I slowly moved away from where Will was still collecting himself. If I got her far enough away, he'd have time to hide.

I held my hands up and waved them, trying to keep her attention and doing my best to show her I wasn't a threat. "I'm not goin' to hurt you. I swear."

"Is that why you kidnapped me from my coven and tortured me for the past few days?"

And Flint thought the *homo magus* were monsters? He was the only monster around here. "That wasn't me, but if we work together, we might be able to make it out of here alive."

"Why would I work with someone who has devoted his entire life to destroying me and my kind?"

"Because I don't want to destroy you or any other member of the magical community." I lowered my hands and my voice, trying to use my soft tone to calm her down. "In fact, I've been doin' everythin' I can to help save the magical community."

Her arched eyebrows told me she didn't believe a word that was coming out of my mouth. "Why would you do something like that?"

That was the simplest answer of all, and it resided in the arms and the eyes of the boy who meant more to me than anything else in the world. "Because I'm in love with a warlock."

She eyed the silent crowd watching us before returning her attention to me. "Liar!"

A powerful stream of water flew out of her hands, heading straight for me. Surprise stole her anger from her expression when the torrent passed harmlessly through me as if I wasn't even there.

The crowd around me roared as if they were watching the Super Bowl, and the witch hunter I had fought so hard to suppress advanced, spurred on by the rallying chant. He grabbed the mental image of Mason, the one that gave me the strength to keep on fighting, and ripped it to shreds. There was no fricking way I was going to allow that to continue. After several deep breaths, I forced him back down into my subconscious. When I had him properly restrained, I returned my attention to the young witch, who had taken several steps away from me.

"*Propellit.*" Instead of flinging me backward as it had done to the guards, her spell had no effect. I remained right where I was. "What are you? Why are my spells not working on you?"

"That doesn't matter." I slowly decreased the distance between us. "We can still get out of this. Together."

She narrowed her eyes. "Or you can die." With a gesture and one word in Latin, the wall to her left tore out of the floor and flew at me.

My mind raced and instinct took over. I dove to the left, underneath the soaring wall, rolled into a ball, and then sprang forward into a sprint.

The witch cursed at me, and more objects suddenly flew in my direction. I evaded a barrel by leaping at a wall, kicking off it, and grabbing one of the rings that hung from the suspended pipes overhead. The inertia carried me up to a raised platform a few feet above where she stood.

She fired off another water stream and followed it with two more barrels. She wasn't letting up, not giving me the opportunity to think beyond the defensive, but I didn't need to think. My body knew exactly what to do.

I flipped off the platform. The wall sailed over me by an inch, but instead of avoiding the barrels that followed it, I landed on the one closest to me and pushed off it. The momentum carried me toward a wall, and the barrel collided with the one behind it, sending them both crashing to the floor and away from me.

I pulled myself up the wall just as another barrel struck where I'd been hanging. I leaped off the wall, caught another dangling ring, and swung myself feetfirst onto the witch.

The collision sent her flying onto her back. I rolled into my landing before springing to my feet.

The crowd watching us exploded with cheers and applause, and I suddenly felt taller, stronger, more powerful than ever.

She shook her head, wiping the small spot of blood from her lips, and glared up at me. I hadn't wanted to fight her, but she left me no choice. Maybe now she'd listen to reason.

"My spells might not work on you." She pointed at Will, who leaned against one of the walls, his mouth agape as he watched me with a mixture of awe and confusion. "But they work on him."

"Please. Don't." I made a move forward, but her waggling finger stopped me.

"Make one move and I'll kill him."

"Think again, you bitch!"

Our gazes snapped back to Will. A sneer twisted his features as he pointed a pistol at the witch. Had he had it this entire time? Before I could get out one word, the muzzle exploded fire, and she fell back onto the ground with a hole in her forehead.

A roar of victory thundered all around me, but those voices slowly faded away. The witch's cold, dead eyes held my complete attention, and I fell to my knees beside her body. I glanced up at Will. The anger had drained from his features as he glanced between the corpse and me. The gun trembled in his hand, and tears welled in his eyes.

"What have I done?" he whispered.

I wasn't certain, but I suspected this was all a part of my uncle's plan.

"YOU LIED to me!" Will railed at his father as he supervised the removal of the witch's body. I couldn't move from the ground where I still knelt.

Flint cast a sideways glance at his son. "And just how did I lie to you?"

"Are you fucking kidding me? You said you were an art collector or some shit."

"I *am* an art collector." He picked up the weapons he'd offered me and gave them to one of his men. "Being a witch hunter doesn't exactly pay the bills. When I'm not killing these vermin, I'm doing exactly what I always told you I did—procuring priceless art."

"But that's not who you are." Will balled his fists into his hair. "You've been living this whole other life that I know jack shit about."

"And whose fault is that?" Flint's voice dropped to barely a whisper.

"Don't you blame this on me." Will stood toe-to-toe with him. "We're witch hunters, magic exists, and you *never* thought to clue me in?"

Flint placed a hand on Will's chest and gently pushed him back. "While I appreciate your passion, something I haven't seen one sign of in eighteen years, I recommend you get ahold of yourself before I knock you on your ass."

Will blew out a lungful of air to calm himself down.

"I haven't told you because being a witch hunter, whether you are born into it or not, is a calling. It's not something you suddenly decide to be. It's in your blood, in your soul. That's why I put you in that cage, to see if it would surface, and it did."

Was that why I'd been having those dreams? Had the witch hunter within me been trying to break free? That would explain my anger in the dream when I killed Mason—Finlay—or the overwhelming sense of brotherhood the cheering crowd had stirred within me just a few moments before. Was I really like my uncle Flint? Was I a cold-blooded killer of the community to which my new family and friends in Havenbridge belonged?

"I wasn't sure you had it in you." Flint placed his hands on Will's shoulders and gave them a big squeeze. "But you do. Otherwise you wouldn't have killed that witch the way you did."

"Why does that make you happy?" Will shook off his father's touch. His lips trembled and he appeared to be three seconds away from spilling the contents of his stomach onto his father's black combat boots. "I just *murdered* someone."

Flint waved his words away. "What you did isn't murder. Do you call it murder when you poison a rat? Is it murder when you gun down a rabid dog?"

Will gulped and shook his head.

"That witch and her kind aren't human. They're a blight upon humanity."

"*You* are the blight upon humanity." My words came out low and sharp as I rose to my feet. Flint regarded me with a cocky grin and crossed arms while Will darted his gaze between us, clearly uncertain what he was supposed to do. "She was innocent. She didn't deserve to be tortured or killed, but you don't care about that. None of you do." I spun around and screamed at the others, who stopped what they were doing to stare at me. "You take the lives of people whose only crime is bein' born different from the rest of us. How can you possibly think that's the right thing to do?"

"Because we know the truth." Flint mimicked my gesture and pointed to the crowd. "*We* know our history as witch hunters. We've embraced who we are. We haven't been brainwashed by lies the way you have."

"Brainwashed? No one has brainwashed me."

Flint looked at me as if I were a silly child. "Really? Then you know that when the *homo magus* first evolved, countless men, women, and children were slaughtered while the warlocks, witches, and wizards battled each other for dominance."

"They didn't kill them on purpose. Yes, they were a warrin' race, but what happened was—"

"Collateral damage?" Flint raised an eyebrow. "That sounds like something a *homo magus* would say, don't you think? They didn't care about humans when they first realized what they were or what they could do. All they cared about was themselves, about being the most powerful. We were no more than cattle to them."

"Fuck." Will furrowed his brow and sneered at the spot where the witch's dead body had been. "Is that how they all are?"

"Don't listen to him." I crossed over to Will and grabbed him by the shoulders, forcing him to look into my eyes. I didn't like the curl to his lip. It reminded me of his father. "He's alterin' the past to fit his agenda."

"Am I?" Flint snapped his fingers, and a soldier trotted over, carrying a book. He handed it to me. *The Origin of the Homo Magus* was embossed in gold across the front of the leather binding. "*That* is the history of the *homo magus* told from a human's perspective. It details how their kind infiltrated the first tribes, inciting wars that brought death and destruction. It provides firsthand accounts of how they seduced humans into marriage and created the abomination they call sorcerers and how those sorcerers turned innocent humans into monsters. And those fairy tales you read as a child, they're in there too, except they aren't made-up stories. They are real-life narratives of confrontations with witches and goblins and trolls and werewolves that spanned generations. Our species was being slowly decimated by their kind for centuries until we started to fight back."

"Holy shit!" Will snatched the book from my hands and flipped it open.

I had half a mind to pluck it out of his grasp. Whatever his father was planning on doing to me was succeeding with Will. "And why should I believe anythin' you say or anythin' that's in this book?"

Flint broke eye contact and sighed. "But you'll believe what your warlock and his family tell you? You'll believe what you've read in *their* books? How is that fair, Mat—Drake? You read their history, listened to their version of our history. Why won't you do the same for us, for other humans, or for the family whose blood rushes through your veins?"

Will glanced up at me, interested in my answer. What could I say? Flint was right. I hadn't heard both sides of the story.

"Humans are in grave danger, Drake. You know it because you've seen it."

I couldn't deny that either. Vampyren were out there, dark fae longed to get back into our world, and Icarian planned to bring life as we knew it to an end with the Spell Fall. While the magical community had their abilities and their spells to defend themselves, humans didn't have that luxury. In fact, most didn't even realize the danger they faced.

Flint patted my shoulder and gave it a squeeze, apparently believing he was winning me over. He obviously believed my daddy raised a fool. "Join us. *Help* us protect humanity from extinction. With your abilities, we can erase magic from existence once and for all."

Which was exactly what the Spell Fall would do. "Is that why you're workin' with Icarian?"

A grin teased up the corners of Flint's mouth as he surveyed the confused expressions of the few men and women still in the cage with us. This was evidently news to them, so why did he not seem bothered by my reveal?

"I was on Aeaea. We both know the witch hunters had infiltrated the island and were workin' with Ben and Sersie. We both also know that *they* took their orders from Icarian." I paused, letting that information sink in. "If you are in charge here, that means *you*, a witch hunter, are workin' with and takin' orders from a magical bein', which represents everythin' you hate." A low murmur spread around us. "Why is that, Uncle Flint?"

His cocky grin pressed into a flat line. "I don't take orders from anyone."

"So what? You think you and Icarian are partners? So did Ben and Sersie. Look where that got them."

"You think you know everything, don't you?" His smile made a reappearance, except this time it was even more devious than before. "That's the trouble with your generation. This is war, and sometimes in war, the enemy of your enemy is your friend."

How could he believe that? Icarian used those around him like expendable chess pieces. "Icarian isn't your friend. He's usin' you, and when he has what he needs, he'll kill you."

Flint laughed as if I'd told the funniest joke he'd ever heard. "Of course he will, but he won't succeed. Icarian and I have… an agreement, and as long as our goals are aligned, we have a truce. When and if that ends, I'll make sure to end him before he has time to strike."

He was mad and had a supersized ego to boot. Icarian possessed incredible power. He could squash Flint and the rest of the witch hunters like bugs. Why didn't Flint see that? "And you think you're a match for him? What makes you so different from all the other bodies in his wake?"

He nodded, and the guards from earlier flanked me. "Because we have you."

"You don't *have* me. You're holdin' me. There's a difference."

"Perhaps right now, but that will soon change once you understand what that dream you've been having means."

The guards once again wrapped their meaty paws around my arms. "If it's so important to you and you know what it means, why don't you just tell me?"

He strutted over to me and grinned like a deranged clown. "I'll do you one better than that. I'm gonna show you."

CHAPTER 12

AFTER ANOTHER quiet march across the compound, Flint and his men led me to the only building in a remote area of the base, far away from where we had started. It stood three stories high and was modern in design with many large windows and a shiny, metallic façade. It was extremely different from the utilitarian Quonset huts that squatted on most of the property. This building was elegant, almost regal, and most likely was the home base of the Orion Group.

Flint nodded at the guards at the entrance, who quickly opened the doors to let us pass. Inside, our footsteps clicked off the shiny, ivory, ceramic floor tiles that branched off into hallways on the right and the left and down the central main corridor, where more armed guards stood in front of the only elevator.

Several paintings decorated the hallway leading to it. One depicted a scene set in Salem during the witch trials. Several Puritan men and women pointed judgmental fingers at a woman who stood before them, quaking in fear. Another showed four women worshiping a half-goat, half-man monstrosity while men carrying pistols surrounded them. The final portrait was of a woman with lavender eyes standing amid beasts that snarled at the viewer. That had to be a rendition of Sersie and her spell that created the first shifters.

One of the elevator guards pushed the button, and by the time we walked up, the doors had already slid open. White marble walls made up the interior. The buttons on the inside were missing. Flint pressed his hand against a small glass panel, which sparked to life upon contact. The digital screen read his fingerprints. After it had verified his identity, the doors shut.

Flint uttered the word "basement," and the elevator descended.

The doors opened to a small, brightly lit foyer where more guards waited. They eyed me before glancing up at Flint and standing at attention. He passed them without acknowledgment and proceeded to another door with another glass panel. He repeated the process from the elevator, and the door opened upon a dark, cavernous room.

The flickering light of computer screens revealed little of the room's contents other than the two people sitting at the row of terminals up ahead. They turned to see who had entered their sanctuary, and upon seeing Flint, they stood and cleared a path between him and the computers.

Flint marched up to the main terminal. His fingers flew across the keyboard, and a second later, a wall-sized screen came to life. The only image visible was the Orion Group insignia. He turned around and smiled. "It is time."

Tension filled the room in a cloud of sweat and the bitter tang of fear. The soldiers next to me tensed, darting their gazes around the room. The people who had been at the computers put more distance between themselves and us. What the heck were these witch hunters expecting? Whatever it was, it wasn't good.

I didn't flinch. I didn't want my uncle to think he was getting the better of me. "Time for what?"

"The truth."

"What does this place have to do with the meanin' of my dream?"

A sound that held no joy exploded from his throat. "Your dream is but a small portion of the truth."

"And what is it?" Will suddenly stood at my side. I couldn't tell if it was a gesture to let me know he had my back or simple curiosity that made him step forward. "You've kept so much from the both of us already."

He nodded. "But now you're *both* ready." He pressed a button on the screen and an image of Mason suddenly appeared. Except it wasn't Mason, at least not the Mason I loved. This man was several years older, perhaps in his thirties, and he wore clothing that looked to last have been in fashion during the 1920s.

I held my breath. "Is that Finlay Appleton?"

Flint applauded. "Well done."

"That's not Finlay Appleton." Will pointed at the screen. "That's Mason. A badly dressed Mason, but that's him."

Another newspaper clipping appeared on the screen. The headline read *Finlay Appleton Dead at 34*. A different photo of Finlay accompanied the article that described how his body was discovered in a remote corner of Bayswater, and that he had died from several gunshots to the chest.

I stumbled backward and my legs gave out. Fortunately Will caught me before I fell to the ground.

"Drake, are you okay?"

I was as far from okay as anyone could be. So many questions jumbled around in my brain and created a traffic jam upon my lips. All I was able to get out was "H-how?"

"We'll get to that in a minute." He waited until Will sat me in a chair before bringing up another image. This time my face graced the screen, and like the previous image of Mason, I looked like myself, but an older version.

Will's mouth hung open. "Drake, that's you."

"Not quite." Flint brought an obituary for Fredrick Croft onto the screen.

As soon as I saw the name, flashes of a life I never lived pooled up from my memories. I remembered growing up on a farm in Hertfordshire. My parents' names were Thomas and Lily. I also had a brother named Sebastian. I attended King's College, where I played cricket. After college I got a job as an accountant in London, where I met Finlay. We became friends and then lovers until I realized he was a warlock and he learned I was a witch hunter. Shortly after that, we killed each other.

"You remember now. Don't you?" Flint crossed over to where I sat and gazed down at me, a triumphant grin stretched wide across his lips.

I recalled more than just my time as Frederick Croft. Memories of other lives Mason and I had lived across the centuries crashed upon the shores of my consciousness. We were in Germany after World War II, Mexico during the Spanish Conquest, France during the Napoleonic Wars, and countless other locations I couldn't quite place. The images were coming too fast, and I was on the verge of blacking out.

"Remember what?" Will rubbed the base of his neck and walked over to the screen to study the image more closely. "What the hell is going on?"

That was what I wanted to know. How was any of this even possible?

That was when the answer hit me. Mason and I were spell bound, two souls tied together throughout our past lives. We lived as lovers, died, and were reborn as two men who would find each other and fall in love all over again. That was what we were told, what we were led to believe. But that wasn't the story that played out in my memories.

"Will someone answer my question?" Will practically screamed.

"I can't." Flint studied me carefully. "Drake has to figure it out on his own. It's the only way this can all stop before it's too late."

A fiery heat roared through my body, and my blood pumped loudly in my ears. "You're tryin' to trick me, aren't you?" I exploded from my seat and wrapped my hands around Flint's neck. "Is this part of Icarian's plan? To make me doubt everythin' I believe, everythin' I hold dear?"

"Drake, stop!" Will stood at my side, trying to get me to release my death grip upon his father's throat. The soldiers who had been watching the events unfold in silence suddenly pointed their guns at me.

I let go and shoved Flint hard. He crashed onto the computer terminal, gasping for breath. "Well, it's not goin' to work. I love Mason. I always have and I always will. We're spell bound, and we *always* will be."

Flint rubbed his sore throat, and after his wheezing stopped, he glanced over at me. "I never said you *weren't* spell bound. Did I?"

"Then what are you tryin' to say by showin' me all those lies?"

He struck a key on the computer, and a slew of photos of Mason and me over the course of many years filled the screen. "How can they be lies if you remember each and every one of your past lives? How can they be lies if the proof is staring you right in your face? The two of you *are* spell bound, but it's not your love that ties you together. Think about how you first met. What was the first emotion you experienced together?"

I shook my head, trying to deny the truth that now seemed so obvious. When I first met Mason, I wanted to strangle him. He was infuriating and got on every one of my nerves. "I hated him." The words slipped from my throat in a barely audible whisper.

"Exactly. You and Mason are spell bound, but not as this great love that has been reborn through the ages. The two of you are spell bound as—"

"Enemies." And at that moment, I knew exactly what my uncle wanted me to do. "You want me to kill him, don't you?"

In reply, Flint placed a pistol in my hand. "Abso-fucking-lutely."

The cool metal of the gun kissed my flesh like a forgotten lover, seducing me to embrace what I was and fulfill the role I had played for more years than I could remember. But I wasn't Frederick Croft or any of the other men I'd once been. I was a new me, a different me. I was Drake Carpenter, and I loved Mason Blackmoor. "I can't."

"You *can*. I know you have what it takes to save us all."

I glanced sideways at him, his words resparking a hate-filled blaze within me. "Then take me to him. Right now."

FLINT DEPARTED with some of his men to fulfill my request and get Mason ready, leaving Will and me alone with two armed guards. The soldiers who had been at the computer terminals before we arrived resumed their stations. What were they doing?

"Are you really going to do it?" Will shoved his hands into his armpits. "Are you really going to kill Mason?"

I eyed the guards. The one with the mustache on the right seemed more interested in chatting with one of the women at the terminal than watching over us. The other guard, the one with a two-inch scar on his forehead, never took his eyes off us. He was going to be a problem. "That's what I said, isn't it?"

"How are you not freaking out right now?" Will paced the length of the room, which caused Scarface to shift his attention from me to Will. "I'm freaking out!"

"I can tell." And I couldn't be more pleased. I traced the engraved lines of the dragon claw in the butt of the gun that rested in my lap. Feeling its cool kiss calmed my turbulent soul. With this weapon, I could accomplish anything. All I needed was the right opportunity.

"I still can't believe magic fucking exists. Who would ever believe this shit?" Will flailed as he continued to wear a hole in the floor. His reaction didn't surprise me. What did surprise me was how long it took for it all to sink in. When I had learned magic first existed, I practically went comatose. It had been Mason's love and his patience that made everything seem not quite as scary. "Yesterday I was your average high school dumbass, worrying about my grades and wondering if I might make Miranda my bae. Today I was almost killed by a witch who shot water out of her hands like she was some kind of fire hose."

Well, at least now I knew I'd only been unconscious for one day. That meant wherever this compound was had required only a short plane trip to get to. With any luck, the Blackmoors had already scried for our location and were on their way. "I know. I was there."

"Yeah, you were. You were jumping all over the place like a jackrabbit on crack. How the hell did you do that?"

"Parkour." I noticed Scarface was growing bored by our conversation. He relaxed his stance and glanced over at his friend, who was still busy flirting.

"Parkour?" Will furrowed his eyebrows. "That was more than just parkour, and you know it. Dad said you're some kind of special witch hunter. Is that why you can do that?"

Yeah. Like I'd take Flint Hopkins's word for anything. He'd just proved how much of a farce all this was. He didn't know I had it figured out. "If that's what your dad says, then I guess so."

Will's eyes suddenly grew wide. "I wonder if I can do that too. I'm a witch hunter, and we're cousins, aren't we? Maybe I can learn."

That seemed highly unlikely. There was something that made me different from every other human and witch hunter. It went beyond my immunity to magic and my ability to avoid spells. I had no clue what that was, but instead of saying all that, all I said was "Maybe."

"I still can't wrap my head around the fact that we're cousins. Even after everything I've seen, *that's* what freaks me out the most, you know?"

I did know. What I didn't know was whether I could trust Will. While my gut told me he had nothing to do with what was going on, the way he killed that witch and how he reacted to his father's words made me doubt what he was going to do once I made my move. "And you didn't know about me, about any of this, before today?"

"Hell no! One minute you and Mason are passed out on the floor in my house, and the next these guys storm in, pointing their guns at the two of you. I almost shit myself until my dad started barking orders and they carried you out of my house and into a black van. The next thing I know, I'm shoved into a different car and then boarding a private jet to

Texas. I had no clue you were even here until those guys put me in that cage with you."

He seemed to be telling the truth. He answered questions as he always did: with more commentary than was necessary. Maybe I could trust him. He might even help me. If he didn't, how was I going to handle that?

Will stood in front of me, pointing at the gun I still held in my lap. "Do you really think you can do it?"

I had to fight the urge to give him a big hug. He gave me just the opportunity I needed by standing directly between Scarface and me, blocking me from view. "We're about to find out."

"What do you mean?" Will's pinched expression quickly turned to shock once I shoved him out of the way.

I fired off a round, hitting Scarface in the chest. He crumpled to the ground while Mustache and his lady reached for their guns and fired back. Instinct once again kicked in, charting a path out of the line of fire. I dove to the right and rolled out of the way as bullets slammed into the chair where I'd been sitting. When I came to a stop, I fired two shots that hit their mark. I trained the barrel of the gun on the last computer tech and clicked back the hammer. "Don't make me shoot you. You've already seen that I don't miss."

He glanced at the bodies to his left and nodded.

Will looked up from where he had curled into a ball on the floor. "What the hell are you doing?"

"Gettin' out of here." I motioned to the gun in the man's holster. "Take your gun out slowly and slide it over here."

He did as I instructed. I picked it up and opened the chamber to see if it was loaded. It was.

"But you said…." Will's voice came out as a squeak. I felt sorry for him. He had no real clue what was going on or what kind of a man his father was. I just had to hope he would grow up to be someone better than Flint Hopkins could ever be.

"I lied." Facing the man, who once more had his hands up in surrender, I nodded for him to sit. He quickly complied. "Bring up whatever you've been workin' on onto the screen."

He turned around but then glanced over his shoulder. "But—"

"Do it!" I pressed the muzzle of the gun to the back of his head.

His fingers flew across the keys, and seconds later, security feeds from within the base flashed before me. Soldiers sat eating lunch in the mess hall where we'd started. Other feeds showed various shots of the perimeter, the grounds, and the rooms of the building we were in. This was the surveillance hub of the Orion Group, which would give me the information I needed. "Show me where you're keepin' the prisoner."

"Which one?"

The man's answer made me snarl. "*All* of them."

Once again his fingers danced across the keyboard. A few moments later, men and women in cages similar to the one from earlier filled the screen.

Will stood at my side, gazing up at the images of bloodied and broken people. "Oh my God. How many of them are there?"

Too many, as far as I was concerned, but there was only one I could focus on right now. I scanned the images until I found him lying in what looked like a hospital room, unconscious. Judging from the windows, Mason was somewhere upstairs in this building. "Where is that?"

The guard followed my finger to the box containing Mason's image. "Room 304."

"Thank you." I swung the butt of the gun at the back of his head. He slumped forward onto the terminal, unconscious.

Will backed up. "Are you going to kill me?"

"No." I crossed over to him and held out my hand in peace. "And I'm not goin' to kill Mason either."

He eyed my hand but didn't take it. "My dad said he's a monster, that he and his kind will kill us all."

"Are you serious?" I pointed to the monitors containing images of dozens of prisoners that had obviously suffered through days of torture. "The only monster is your father and the rest of the people in this place."

Will's face flushed as he batted my hand away. "Don't talk about my dad that way. You don't know shit about him."

Neither did Will, not really, but Flint was his father, and he and I didn't share the same history they did. "No, I don't. You know him better than I do."

"That's right. I *do*. That's why I believe him when he says we're fighting for our survival. That witch tried to kill me, and I bet she's no better than any of the rest of them."

The world wasn't as black and white as Flint and Will saw it. "Just like you know your father better than I do, I know Mason, his family, and so many other magical people better than any of you. I've seen the love in their hearts. I've witnessed how they've done their best to protect *everyone*, human and magical, from threats you couldn't even imagine. Maybe their species started out violently and maybe they didn't care much about humans at first, but they do now. They've learned their lesson. When do you think humans will finally learn theirs?"

Will didn't respond. He met my gaze and didn't look away. Although the storm clouds in his eyes subsided, he wasn't going to help me. He wasn't going to stand in my way either. He motioned to the door we entered. "Go. Before my dad gets back."

There was so much I wanted to say. I wanted to tell him how glad I was to meet him, how given time and better circumstances, we could grow close, but there was no time for that. Mason needed me, and I had to get to him, fast.

With one final nod at Will, I sprinted out the door and toward the boy of my past, present, and future.

AFTER, I used the speed and dexterity I'd been gifted with to quickly take out the surprised guards in the hallway. I grabbed one of the unconscious men by the arm, dragging him over to the elevator and pressing the button. When the doors slid open, I pulled him inside and placed his hand against the security panel, hoping and praying his security clearance would activate the lift. If it didn't, I was screwed.

The doors shut and awaited my command. "Level three."

While the elevator ascended, I grabbed the guard's weapon and tucked it into the waistband of my jeans. I then palmed the other two pistols, ready to come out guns blazing. Although I didn't want to kill anyone, I'd do whatever was necessary to get to Mason.

The elevator doors opened to an empty foyer. I took one tentative step out of the lift, glancing both ways. No guards. No Flint. No noise whatsoever besides the low hum of the air conditioner whooshing through the vents.

My stomach sank. This wasn't right. If Flint had come up here to get Mason ready for me to "kill" him, this floor should be crawling with armed soldiers. Something was up, and I had to be ready for anything.

I exited the elevator, and the doors closed behind me as it headed back to the main floor. I inched my way out of the foyer, peeking into another empty hallway. Closed doors lined both sides of the corridor. Anyone or any*thing* could be in any of those rooms, and I had to go past them all to get to the last one on the right, where Mason was being kept prisoner.

If I took the time to inspect them all, I could lose precious moments finding Mason and getting us both to safety. If I didn't, I might find myself surrounded by armed guards pissed off that I chose Mason over my own kind.

The Drake I was before Mason would have played the safe route, but I wasn't that guy anymore. Being with Mason had changed me, and I *had* become more like him than I realized. After taking several deep breaths, I sprinted down the hallway to room 304.

When no one came out of the rooms behind me and started shooting, I wasn't as relieved as I thought I'd be. I turned the doorknob and found it unlocked. Dread slowly crept up my spine. Something besides Mason waited for me on the other side.

I released the breath I'd been holding and inched open the door, pointing the barrels of both guns into the room. When the door stood all the way open, I couldn't believe what I was seeing. There was supposed to be a hospital-type room on the other side, not a long, gloomy corridor covered in cobwebs. The floor should be shiny, white tile, not rotted wood, and there should be a bed with Mason on it lying in front of the window. There should *not* be a darkened house with shadowy hallways extending into an endless void.

I should *not* be staring into the house from my dream.

CHAPTER 13

As soon as I stepped across the threshold, my vision swam. The world spun around as if I was somehow falling but standing at the same time. It didn't make sense, but if it didn't stop, I was going to lose it all over the wooden floor. I leaned against the moldy wall to avoid falling over, and it took several deep breaths before the world returned to normal.

Well, as normal as the world could be when you find yourself wide-awake and face-to-face with a scene from one of your worst nightmares. Wait. Was I awake? I slapped my face hard, and a stinging burn spread like fire across my cheek. The shadowy interior didn't suddenly change into my bedroom at Blackmoor Manor or the hospital room I'd seen on the monitor in the basement.

I had to be awake, and this had to be real, somehow.

The door slammed shut behind me, and I jumped. Grasping at the knob, I turned and pulled it, trying to get it open, but it wouldn't budge. It was sealed shut.

Once again facing the shadows before me, I inched my way farther into the darkened corridor I had traveled in my dream. The same black-and-brown mold dotted the ceiling, and the familiar stench of rotting wood burned my nasal cavities. The rooms to my left and right remained empty except for the shroud of shadows, and the faint moonlight once again cast an eerie glow onto the floors.

But as similar as the scene was, there were also notable differences. For one, the door behind me didn't have a hole in it from where I kicked it in. I wasn't wearing tan-and-cream two-tone shoes, and I was carrying two pistols, with one tucked into the crook of my back. This told me I wasn't in my dream-memory from my past life as Frederick Croft. I was me, and this was happening right now.

So how did I get here? Had I walked through a portal connecting the Orion Group compound to this house? If that was the case, there was only one person I could think of who would be responsible for casting such a spell.

Icarian.

"You finally made it." It was strange hearing our unknown enemy speak for the first time, but not as strange as his tone. His words drifted around me as if he were talking through a speaker, which added an odd but familiar mechanical tone to his voice. Despite the strange timbre, I'd expected him to sound like some comic book villain who either cackled maniacally or spoke in a booming, gloom-laden tone. Other than the fact I couldn't see him, he seemed rather... normal.

Still, I wasn't going to let the average-joe tone of his voice drop my guard. Even though it would likely do me no good against someone with power that rivaled the Conclave's, I pulled back the hammers of both pistols and surveyed the darkness. "Yeah, sorry about that. Your hired thugs detained me."

His laughter echoed throughout the house as if we were old friends watching our favorite sitcom. "I told Flint his plan wouldn't work, but he believed he could sway you." I moved into the house as he spoke, pointing my guns into the shadowed rooms before moving farther down the corridor. "He actually believed you'd choose him and your lineage because you were related."

The casual flair of the conversation unnerved me. Although I hated to admit it, I'd prefer for him to be cackling maniacally. That wouldn't creep me out as much. "He was wrong." I moved along the wall, keeping the final doorway in sight while peeking toward the foyer that opened up to the staircase. "He's also a psychopath."

"Clearly." The voice followed me as if Icarian was strolling right beside me. My breath hitched, and I swung out with the butts of the guns. That made him laugh louder. "Although it might sound as if I'm right next to you, I'm not, but I am closer than you might think."

That sure didn't make me feel any better. "Then why don't you show yourself?" I peered into the final room, the one where Finlay had shot me—well, Frederick—in the stomach with his scarlet energy. Seeing it empty, I continued toward the staircase. "Are you afraid?"

"Don't be ridiculous." Apparently that comment was even funnier than wildly swinging at empty air. "I have nothing to fear from you."

No matter how casual he attempted to be, I didn't buy that for a minute. Somehow, some way, I was an obstacle for Icarian and his plan. Otherwise, why would he go through all this trouble to try to place Mason and me at odds? He gained something from one or both of our deaths. I had to figure out exactly what that was. "Is that why you used my aunt Millie against me?"

His laughter ceased, and silence thicker than a San Francisco fog rolled into the room for several moments. "Although I'm not surprised, you must tell me how you figured that out."

"You mean when did I realize it wasn't my aunt Millie who begged me to kill her in her basement?"

"Yes." The strangely cheery tone of his voice had me imagining him with his elbows on a table, chin on his palms, leaning in closer for the reveal.

"When Flint told me I could kill Mason, he said I had 'what it takes to save us all.' Those were the exact words Aunt Millie said after I put a stake through her heart. That's when it clicked and I realized I was bein' played. It was too coincidental. He'd either been there when it happened or knew someone who was. The only one who that could have been was you."

"I'm impressed."

He actually did sound impressed, which freaked the fool out of me. Still, he didn't deny it. That meant my aunt Millie was still alive and waiting for me to save her. I glanced up the stairs, but I couldn't see past the top landing. Inky cloaks of darkness spread out like a blanket across the second floor. "Why did you do it, and why bring me here?"

"Isn't it obvious? I wanted to lead you to the truth. You and Mason have always believed yourselves to be connected by a never-ending love." This time the amusement in his voice made my upper lip curl. "Well, at least until you discover that the two of you are bitter rivals that have hunted and killed each other across more lifetimes than you can recall. You are spell bound as enemies. It's your destiny to find and kill each other."

I wouldn't accept that. While Mason and I might have been enemies in the past, it didn't mean it was our destiny to remain locked in mortal combat. After all, magic lived in the world; anything was possible. But Icarian's answer got me thinking. "If Mason and I always discover the truth on our own, why intervene? Why not just let it happen if it's really supposed to happen?"

"Because whether you believe it or not, I'm not the bad guy here. I'm actually trying to fix a horrible flaw. I do *not* want to bring about the Spell Fall. In fact, I've been doing everything possible to prevent it."

That didn't make any sense. Icarian had been using Ben and Sersie to collect the Crests of the Five for the sole purpose of ending all magic. If he didn't really want that, why go through all the trouble in the first place? "You're right. I don't believe you. You've been tryin' to kill me, Mason, and his brothers since I first arrived in Havenbridge. Everythin' you've done has been an attempt to murder us or to steal one of the crests."

"Oh, Drake." His chuckle was starting to tick me off. "I haven't been trying to murder you. Well, at least not directly. Have you been in danger? Yes, but that's mostly because of Ben and Sersie. They wanted revenge for all the wrongs they believed had been heaped upon them. Those poor, pitiful souls. What they needed was a good therapist, not revenge, but what could I do? They were a means to an end, so I gave them free rein to do what needed to be done as long as they either retrieved the crests or killed one of the Blackmoor brothers. After all, stealing the crests for the Spell Fall has always been plan B."

It took me a few minutes to process the information. If killing Mason, Thad, or Pierce was plan A, then that meant—

"Are you sayin' Mason and his brothers are the reason you're tryin' to end magic? That if they die, then all of this would be over?"

"Like I said, it's not necessary for them all to die. One would certainly suffice, and if that happened, everything would go back to the way it was."

His matter-of-fact attitude that murder was the solution told me Icarian was even more certifiable than Ben, Sersie, and Uncle Flint combined. Why would their deaths be an answer to anything? While Mason and his brothers were ornery and sometimes rude, they had big hearts and had done so much to protect magic *and* humans. "This is a trick of some kind. It has to be."

Another hearty chuckle reverberated in the walls. "If only it was. I want you to think about something. The Blackmoor brothers have tapped into abilities far beyond those of ordinary warlocks. Not only can Pierce command electricity, but he can now see auras and turn into living lightning. *That* has never occurred in all of recorded magical history. On

Otherworld, Thad tapped into the magic of the fae, a feat that has never before been accomplished, and Mason—"

"Is the first shadow weaver in over five hundred years."

"Precisely. On their own in separate covens at different points in time, this would be an anomaly not worthy of concern, but these are three brothers in the present. They have upset the fragile balance of magic, and if it is allowed to continue, their powers will only grow, further fracturing the delicate foundation of life and bringing forth the long-forgotten Prophecy of the Three. For the greater good, I cannot allow this to occur. In order to save all of magic and all of creation from the tyranny they will bring, either magic must end or a Blackmoor brother must die. It's really that simple."

If it was that simple, then it begged the question: "Why use me, or Ben, or Sersie? Why not just kill one of them yourself?"

"Because I… can't." The guilt and remorse in his suddenly hesitant voice didn't make sense.

"Why the hell not? You're supposed to have all this power. Why make others do your dirty work for you?"

The deafening silence told me I wouldn't be getting an answer, which meant there was another piece to this already complicated puzzle. It also made me question a truth we'd all taken for granted—that Icarian was our enemy's name. After all, it hadn't been Aunt Millie who had provided me with the information in the basement. It had been Icarian. He was too smart to make himself vulnerable by revealing his identity.

If that was true, who *was* Icarian? It was an answer I wouldn't find right now.

Whether Icarian, or whoever he was, was telling the truth about this prophecy or any of his reasons, I didn't care. Mason and his brothers were not capable of turning into the monsters Icarian predicted they'd be. *I* wouldn't let that happen and neither would Aiden or Kale. The Blackmoors' love had saved us over the past few months, and it was our turn to save them.

Icarian might not be motivated by evil, but he was acting out of fear. That was deadlier than anything Mason, Thad, or Pierce could ever do or become. "You're lyin' to me and to yourself. You're afraid of them. That's the only reason you're doin' all this. Admit it."

The house rattled as if it had been lifted off its foundation and slammed back down. The walls to my left groaned as large cracks spread out along the drywall, and chunks of ceiling rained down all around me.

"Did I hit a nerve?"

"Not at all." The timbre in his voice had changed. His casual demeanor had been replaced by a sense of urgency. What the heck was going on now? "But it's time to bring this to an end."

I couldn't agree more. "Tell me where Mason is."

"Where he's always been." The smile in his voice was unmistakable. "Right behind you."

I spun around and a figure, draped in shadows, stood in front of the door at the opposite end of the corridor.

"Mason?" In response to my words, the shape silently glided down the corridor, and I retreated until my back pressed against the far wall. I raised my pistols with trembling hands.

"He remembers your past." Icarian's words weighed heavy on the air around me. "He *always* remembers right after you do, and he *will* kill you. The only way to save yourself is to kill him first."

His words seeped into my brain, tugging on the inner witch hunter, who struggled to be free. He wanted to crawl out from his depths, he longed to kill Mason as he had done for years, because to that part of me, death was the answer to everything. But he was wrong. There was another way. There was *always* another way, and with the love for Mason I still clung to inside my heart, I would find it. I lowered the pistols to my sides.

"What are you doing?" If I could see Icarian, I had no doubt his mouth would be agape. "You have to defend yourself. You've relived your past. You know what will happen if you don't."

Instead of responding to him, I focused my attention straight ahead. "Mason, are you okay? Talk to me."

He drifted before me, held aloft by shadows that bubbled like tar beneath him. They reminded me of the darkness Ben had commanded. This was an ability Mason hadn't mastered before. His powers were growing just like Icarian said they would. "You want an answer?" A crazed grin slashed its way across his features, and the flaming pyre of hate I remembered from my dream gazed down at me. "Then how about this one? I'll be okay once you're dead."

FOR SEVERAL moments I stood there, unable to speak. No matter what our pasts might be, I refused to believe Mason could be coerced into killing me. There wasn't any spell powerful enough to break the bond we shared. Something else was going on, something I couldn't see.

"Drake."

A voice drifted around me, but it wasn't Icarian's. Whoever was speaking sounded as if they were calling my name underwater.

"Who is it? Who's there?"

Before I got a reply, Mason erupted in a cry of fury.

Seconds before a shadow blast ripped the wall behind me apart, I sprinted to the right, leaped over a shadowy tentacle that reached out for my legs, and darted into the next room. No matter what I hoped or believed, like Finlay, Mason wanted to kill me, and my love for him made me vulnerable to him. I had to pray the same could still be said in return.

Right now, though, I had to find shelter and a way out of this that didn't involve killing the boy I loved.

The low hum that filled the room told me Mason didn't feel the same way. I rolled to the left as another blast of negative energy obliterated the wall to my right. "Please, stop!"

"Why? So you can kill me?" Misery twisted his voice, and it broke my heart.

I dashed back into the corridor as Mason glided into the room I'd just left behind. "I'd never hurt you. You know that."

The wall to my left exploded, sending me slamming into the other side of the hallway. The pistols fell out of my grasp and slid across the floor. Clouds of plaster filled my lungs and a trailing warmth spilled over my right cheek. I ran my fingers across my temple, and when I pulled them back, they were covered in blood.

"Drake, can you hear me?"

There it was again. Unlike Icarian's voice, which floated electronically on the air, this one seemed to be coming from within me. How was that possible?

"You're a witch hunter." Mason's venom yanked me back to my current predicament. He glided slowly toward me like some deranged serial killer in a horror movie. "You've killed me in every one of our past lives. What makes *this* one so different?"

"This is different. This isn't like before."

Both Mason and the voice were right. This was both different and the same. We had killed each other before, and right now, this scene was playing out almost exactly as it had in my dream-memory. Mason had already wounded and disarmed me, save for the gun still tucked into my waistband. All that was left for us to do was to head upstairs for the final act.

"Do you understand?"

I did. Icarian had orchestrated all this. He had pretended to be Aunt Millie and forced me to "kill" her in order to set me up to take out Mason for what he saw as the "greater good." He'd been hoping *I* would succeed where Ben and Sersie had failed. By killing Mason, I'd remove Icarian's fears and the need for the Spell Fall.

There was only one hitch. Whatever spell Icarian was trying to weave wouldn't work.

It was a clever plan to use my dreams and memories to sidestep my immunity to magic. With my defenses down, it was easy for him to bring forth my inner witch hunter. But now that I knew this dream was also magic, Icarian's ploy was over. My magical immunity would take care of his spell while I used the magic Mason and I created to save him from Icarian's web.

"Answer my question!" In response to Mason's anger, the shadows around me lifted off the walls and turned into pointed spikes. They angled toward where I crouched, ready to turn me into a pincushion.

"You can see it now. Can't you? You can see the difference."

I could, and it was time for Mason to see it too. "You want to know what's different?" I stood up, not focusing on the shadowy weapons that inched their way toward me. They didn't matter anymore. What mattered was the boy who stood in front of me, the one with anger flashing like lightning across his eyes. That wasn't the Mason I knew. The real Mason sat trembling like a child in the eye of the hurricane. The anger and the bravado had always been a mask that hid the insecure boy I loved.

Hot tears rolled down my cheeks, mingling with the blood that still flowed from my wound. Not only did I love Mason, but I wanted Mason and he wanted me. We had desired and found each other across lifetimes.

That was the miracle of our love. That was our legacy, and that was what I was going to force him to see. "I made a promise to you the other day. Do you remember?"

The shadow spikes hesitated for a second. He did remember. "Your promise to love me forever? That was just another one of your lies." Once again the shadow instruments of death inched toward me.

"It wasn't a lie. Nothin' about our lives together has *ever* been a lie. We've always met and we've always fallen in love. That is our truth. But for some reason, Finlay and Frederick and all of our past selves forgot that. They let what we were cloud *who* we were. We are not enemies, Mason. Bein' enemies is a choice. Lovin' you is not." I stepped away from the wall, past the spikes that reached out to me, and toward Mason on his floating black cloud. "I promised to love you forever, and you promised me the same thing. Was that a lie?"

The anger inside him flickered as Mason gazed down at me.

"Yes, you're doing it. Come back to us. Come back."

"No." Icarian's friendly nature crumbled as his cry shook the house like a rag doll, causing walls to come crashing down. "You must fulfill your destiny and kill each other. Sacrifice yourselves for the good of all of life and all of magic."

I stood on my tiptoes and caressed Mason's cheek. His skin trembled against my touch, and the cloud of bubbling shadows that held him aloft lowered him to the ground. The storm Icarian had manipulated within him no longer raged, and the shadows around me slowly retreated to their corners.

The warlock I loved was making his way back to me, but his progress was sluggish. He'd been through a lot. Whatever Icarian had done to him had practically wrung all hope from his soul, but I would bring him back. Our love would give him his legs.

"I love you, Mason Blackmoor." I rubbed my cheek against his, forcing his nose into my neck, where he inhaled deeply. He instinctively moved his hands to my waist and clutched at my flesh. "I will always love you. No matter what."

Mason pulled out of the embrace and gazed down at me with blue eyes brighter than a clear summer day. The raging storm had passed. "And I love you too." A grin teased its way across his plump, juicy lips that I longed to take between my teeth. "Even if you are a witch hunter."

We fell into each other's arms, laughing. In response, the house around us convulsed and fell apart as Icarian's angry screams faded. We had what was important—we had each other—so while the house from my dream continued its death throes, I held on to Mason as tightly as he held on to me.

CHAPTER 14

An explosion jolted me awake, and I found myself on a hospital bed, my arms wrapped around Mason. Even though he was still sound asleep, a goofy grin dangled from his lips as he held me tightly to his chest. God, I wanted him real bad right now.

The entire room shook, and I let out a surprised yelp.

"Thank the Gate. You're awake." Charlotte's voice surprised my erection and me. She stood by the bed, her hands glowing cerulean. Had she been using her water-based healing powers on us? Was hers the voice I'd heard inside the house?

"It's about damn time!" Thad stood before a block of ice that used to be the doorway.

On the other side, Flint and his soldiers were slamming a battering ram against the icy barrier. Anger twisted his expression as he glared at me. It no longer mattered that I was his nephew. If he made it in here, he'd kill me.

Another explosion rocked the building. This time Pierce hovered in front of the window, covered in pink lightning and facing the other direction. Arcs of electricity flew from his fists, striking something on the ground below.

"What the heck is goin' on?"

"You were trapped in dream magic." Beads of sweat dotted Charlotte's brow, and she started to sway. I darted off the bed and grabbed her hand, giving her the support she needed. She grinned at me in thanks before once again standing on her own.

"Dream magic?" Mason's weary voice croaked behind me.

I whirled around, and the sight of his big, dopey grin brought me to tears. "You're okay." I pulled him into my arms and covered his face with kisses.

"Only because of you." He pressed his lips to my cheeks and nuzzled against me. "I couldn't control myself. It was like I was trapped in my own body."

That was precisely what it felt like in all my other dreams, most likely a result of Icarian's manipulation of our dreams and our memories. "That doesn't matter now. All that matters is you're safe."

Gunfire rattled in the hall as the soldiers abandoned their battering ram and riddled Thad's ice wall with bullets.

"Swap spit later," Thad grunted as he refortified the barrier. "We need to get out of here."

"What about Mason?" I asked. He looked like he'd been chewed up, spit out, and stepped on.

"I'll be fine." He attempted to get off the bed, but he could barely sit up. There was no way he was walking out of here.

Charlotte ran her hand over his forehead. "You're too weak. I managed to get most of the hemlock out of your body, but it's still taken its toll. You're lucky to be alive."

Mason scrunched up his lips. "What the fuck is hemlock?"

Thad cursed at his brother's lack of magical knowledge. "We don't have time for this. We need Miranda to warp him out of here."

She can't. Elliot's voice suddenly spoke in our heads, and we all gritted our teeth. Apparently after the Blackmoors realized we were missing, they had called in the cavalry. *She's rescuing the prisoners we found in the compound.*

I was relieved to hear that. Miranda would make sure every single witch, wizard, and warlock made it safely out of this hellhole.

I'll take care of this. That was Adam's voice speaking through Elliot's telepathic link. The wind outside picked up and Adam floated into view, riding his air-based powers all the way to the third floor. He smiled at us from the other side of the window. "Step back."

Charlotte uttered a word in Latin as her brother unleashed a gale-force wind. The shattered glass bounced harmlessly off her protection spell. A second later the four of us were floating out of the building and down to the battleground below.

Mr. Blackmoor thudded across the compound in his stone armor. Bullets ricocheted off him as he sent witch hunters skidding across the pavement. Several screams caught my attention as Mr. Proctor fired bolts of flame into an approaching squadron, corralling them toward a grove of trees. Under Mrs. Proctor's command, the tree limbs came to life, reaching out to wrap their wooden arms around the soldiers, rendering them unable to fight.

Pierce flew above us, zapping snipers with his lightning, while Kale in his eagle form descended on an unlucky soldier. His claws and beak ensured that the man would never be able to fire another gun.

"Kill them!" Flint yelled from the broken window above us.

The men with him aimed their rifles at us, but before they could get off a shot, Aiden, who was in his vampyren form, flew right into them. I couldn't see what Aiden was doing to them, but judging from their screams of torment, it wasn't pleasant.

The captives have been secured. Courtesy of his son's telepathy, Mr. Stonewall's voice blared in my head—and everyone else's, if their winces were any indication. *We're on our way back to you now.*

As I watched my friends and family put the finishing touches on the remaining soldiers, I sank to my knees upon the warm grass surrounding the building. Was this part of our nightmare finally over?

If so, where was the Conclave? They typically arrived once everything was said and done. Their absence sent a shiver down my spine.

"Drake?" Even though he was still extremely weak, Mason managed to walk over to me on unsteady legs and fall onto the ground beside me. "Are you okay?"

Being next to Mason certainly made things better, but as I snuggled into his embrace, one final pang of dread shuddered within my soul.

I LOUNGED in Mason's embrace for several minutes until the Stonewalls, Miranda, and the Edwells returned with the remaining soldiers bound in magical energy. Will was among them. Fear had drained all color from his skin as he darted his gaze at his surroundings, most likely wondering when he was going to be killed.

When he saw me standing with Mason and the others, his fear gave way to the gloomy clouds of anger and resentment. I had to talk to him. I had to get him to understand that choosing to save Mason and my new family didn't mean I was turning my back on him. He was my family too.

I glanced over my shoulder at Mason, who didn't need me to tell him what I wanted to do. He encouraged me with a nod, and his smile told me he'd be waiting for me when I returned.

As I crossed over to where Will and the witch hunters were closely watched by Pierce, Kale, and Adam, the celebratory voices of the others behind me abruptly stopped.

"What are you doing over here?" Kale moved to help me walk. Evidently I appeared weaker than I felt. "You should be resting."

I offered him a smile but declined his assistance with a wave. "I have to talk to Will."

All three of them looked to where I nodded, and their pinched eyebrows communicated their confusion.

Pierce was the first to speak up. "Why do you want to talk to him? He's a witch hunter."

"So am I." He took a step back in response to the tone of my voice. "What's your point?"

"But he's dangerous. Isn't he?" Adam glanced around as if looking for agreement.

"He's about as dangerous as I am." I stood next to Will. The gesture blew some of his storm clouds away. Perhaps our relationship could still be salvaged. "Release him. He isn't responsible for any of this. He's as much of a victim as I am."

Pierce rubbed the back of his neck. "Listen, Drake. I appreciate that you want to help him. He's your family. I get it. But Dad and the other High Priests ordered us to keep them secured."

"Either release him or I will." I held my hand over the mystical energy that kept him bound to the others. "We both know I can do it."

With one glance at Kale and Adam, who reluctantly nodded, Pierce mumbled in Latin and the blue energy that bound Will disappeared.

He rubbed his wrists and eyed me warily as he stepped away from the soldiers behind him, who cursed at me. "Why'd you do that?"

"Because we're family."

Will nodded to the group that was gathering behind us. "I thought *they* were your family."

I glanced over my shoulder at Mason's grinning face and the faces of the people who had become my family. Well, except for the Edwells.

Nobody liked them. All they did was scowl. "They *are* my family." I turned back to Will and squeezed his shoulder. "But so are you."

"Really?" The surprise in his voice made me laugh and broke my heart at the same time. His turbulent relationship with his father had evidently made him an insecure wreck.

"Of course."

"How can you say that? My father drugged, kidnapped, and tried to kill you."

"That's on him, not on you."

Will glanced around the group of magically shackled men and women. "I don't see him anywhere. Where is he?"

That was when I remembered Aiden had flown through the window on the third floor to deal with Flint and the soldiers who had been trying to kill us. Chances were likely he hadn't survived the encounter. "Aiden, what happened to those men you fought?"

Aiden stared at the ground. "I took care of them."

"What does that mean?" Will took two angry steps forward, and everyone clicked on their active powers. "Did you kill him?"

I placed my hands on Will's shoulders and held him back. I didn't want him to do anything that would get him killed. As long as he wasn't trying to actively harm a magical being, magical law prevented all covens from taking a human life. "Will, he was tryin' to kill us."

Will spun around. "And? According to my dad, that's what their kind has done to ours since they first evolved." His response earned him hoots of support from the prisoners and sneers from everyone else. All except Mason. His nod meant the world to me. No matter what, he had my back.

"You saw the horror he was capable of. He made you kill that witch in the cage. I know you don't want to hear this, but Flint Hopkins was a monster."

"That's exactly what he called *them*." Will nodded to Mason and the others and snorted. "You didn't like it when he did that. You came to their defense, and you have the gall to label *my* dad as a monster?"

This was headed in a direction I didn't like. Will was slipping through my fingers, and I had to stop it before he was lost to me forever. "You saw what horror he was capable of. Like you said, he drugged, kidnapped, and tried to kill me."

Will waved my words away. "He never would have killed you. He was trying to *save* you."

"Would he have killed me?" Miranda stepped forward.

When Will saw her, his jaw almost hit the ground. "Y-you're a witch?"

A light blue aura surrounded her, and a second later she warped herself right next to Will. "Does that answer your question?"

Will stumbled away from her as if she had the plague. "I can't believe you're a witch." He covered his mouth. "And I kissed you."

I rolled my eyes. "Bein' a witch doesn't mean she has cooties."

"I would disagree." Mason's commentary earned him a smack upside his head courtesy of Charlotte.

"Will, listen to me." I forced my gaze to his, wanting him to not only hear my words but to feel them. "Are there bad people in the magical community? Yes. Believe me, we've fought enough of them to know. But there are bad people who aren't magical too. No one, whether human or magical, is a monster by birth. The only monsters are the ones who allow themselves to live and act with hate in their hearts."

My words seemed to be working. Burning pyres no longer lit the blue sky of his eyes. They only flickered to life when he glanced over my shoulder at Aiden. "*He* killed my father. As far as I'm concerned, he *is* a monster."

I couldn't imagine how painful that was for Aiden to hear. As a vampyre, he was sensitive to being called a monster. Hopefully Will would change his mind with time. "I understand."

"Well, I don't." A voice boomed in the sky above us.

When I glanced up, I couldn't speak. How was this possible?

Will took a step forward. "Dad?"

Flint floated in the sky, his cocky grin slanting across his lips, and the soldiers cheered their leader's arrival. "It takes more than a vampyre to take me out, son, especially when you've got friends like mine."

A being made entirely of golden radiant light suddenly flickered into view beside my uncle. I shoved past everyone, placing myself between my family and our enemy. "Get back. That's Icarian."

"Now's our chance." Pierce suddenly shifted into his pink lightning form. "We can kill him and end this right now."

The nodding heads around me showed they agreed. A low rumble preceded everyone clicking on their powers at once. Pierce, Kale, Aiden, and Adam took to the sky, streaking straight for Icarian while Mason and the others on the ground took aim, preparing to unleash a volley of magic that would likely split the heavens.

In response, Icarian chuckled. "I find this extremely amusing." Without a gesture or a word, those overhead plummeted to the ground. I watched in horror as my family and friends were pinned to the earth by some unseen immeasurable weight that shut off their powers.

A second later the mystical strands of energy that bound the witch hunters vanished. They picked up the weapons that lay strewn across the grass and concrete before pointing them at the heads of the people I loved.

I rushed over to Mason, moving myself in front of the barrel of the gun that would end his life. "Please, don't do this!"

"Get out of here." Mason gritted his teeth in pain. Icarian's magic was crushing his chest. "Run!"

"What the fuck, Drake? Get out of the way." Will grabbed my hand, trying to force me out from in front of certain death, but I shoved him aside.

"Listen to Will." Mason forced out the words in ragged gasps. "You need to go."

No, I didn't. I was right where I needed to be. Why did Mason always forget we were stronger together than we were apart? He obviously needed a reminder. I placed my hand on Mason's chest, and a moment later, his grimace of pain turned into a devious smile.

"I'm so hot for you right now."

Leave it to Mason to come on to me in the middle of a dangerous situation. "Will you just do your thing already?"

His smile rolled into a full-on grin. "Fine, but when we get home, your ass is mine."

Shadowy tentacles erupted around Mason. The inky limbs quickly disarmed the soldiers around us.

"Fire!" Flint shouted from above, but as the remaining soldiers carried out their order, Mason erected a dome of negative energy, safely protecting us from the hail of bullets.

"That's what I'm fucking talking about," Pierce said through gritted teeth.

Thad groaned in pain. "I'd be more impressed if he could get this weight off our chests before it flattens us."

"Can it, Brainiac." Perspiration dripped down Mason's face as he concentrated on maintaining the barrier under the constant hail of bullets. "I'm busy saving your ass right now."

Flint, who'd been lowered to the ground, opened fire at the barrier. "How the fuck is this possible?" He glanced up at Icarian. "You said you could turn off their abilities."

"I can." The light form that was Icarian glanced at me. "But your nephew, it seems, can cancel out my own."

Damn straight. Besides Mason's, I was immune to all other forms of magic, evidently even the abilities of someone who'd grown just as powerful as the Conclave.

Icarian slowly descended until he hung just above the black dome. I kept both hands on Mason's shoulders, forcing all my willpower on canceling out whatever spell Icarian tossed our way. Although he could use his powers to kill Thad or Pierce, I was banking on his inability to get his hands dirty keeping him from going down that path. If he did travel down that road, there was no way I would be able to protect them without letting go of Mason.

"I see from your death grip that any spell I cast against Mason won't work." Profound disappointment filled his voice.

My muscles tensed as I prepared for the next magical onslaught. "That's right. So you might as well just go home."

"I have no other choice, then." Icarian's right hand glowed with a deep emerald light while flames of red energy licked across his left fist. "I will have to resort to plan B."

Before I had a chance to react, a force tugged upon my chest, violently yanking me out from under Mason's protective dome until I floated in front of Icarian. Mason screamed at me from below, sending the shadowed tentacles at his command out to retrieve me, but before they could reach me, Icarian's power dissipated them.

I struggled against the force that held me in its grasp. "How did you do that? I'm immune to your powers."

"To mine, yes." He nodded to his open glowing hands. "But not to these." In one palm rested an emerald with an open lily across its face. It had once been Aunt Millie's pendant. Now I knew it to be the Earth Crest. In the other hand sat the Hearthstone, a ruby burning with magical fire. That was the Fire Crest, which had once belonged to the fae in Otherworld.

While I wasn't surprised to see them in Icarian's possession, the missing Air Crest puzzled me. Where was it? Hadn't Icarian stolen it from the shifters a few days ago?

"The crests get their power directly from the Gate." Icarian's words tore me out of my thoughts. "There is no defense against their power, and while I wield them, there is no defense against me."

"So what? You're goin' to kill me?"

Icarian's laughter rumbled through the sky. "I've already told you that I mean you no harm."

"Then what are you up to?"

"Plan B."

A cry of pain ripped from my throat when Icarian plunged his hand into my chest.

I LOST all concept of time. I had no idea if it had only been a few seconds or an hour as I floated next to Icarian, his hand piercing my chest. Fire licked across my flesh, and my guts twisted and wrenched as he moved his spectral hand inside me, searching for something.

Whatever it was, I hoped he'd find it quickly. My throat burned from my constant screams, and the coppery taste of blood filled my mouth.

"Hold still. It'll be over in just a moment." He jerked his hand to the left, grazing against my heart, which sputtered. My body convulsed. My hyperventilating lungs worked overtime to drag in as much oxygen as they could to keep me conscious, but the exhausted organs were quickly losing the battle. Icarian said he hadn't wanted to kill me, but he'd brought me right up to the precipice.

"You're dead!" Mason's angry voice crackled through the sky and caught my drifting attention. He sent tentacles of shadows up to where we floated. They struck the golden ball that had been erected around us. When had that happened?

Down below, the shadow barrier Mason had raised to save the others from the witch hunters had fallen. The soldiers were either dead or strung up so tightly they'd no longer be a threat. Their movement told me the rest of the covens had somehow managed to get free of Icarian's spell. In his haste to retrieve whatever he searched for in my body, he must have relaxed his hold on my friends and family.

They were about to make him pay. I just hoped I lived long enough to see Mason kick his ass.

Pink lightning streaked around us, and I knew what that meant. My loved ones were powering up. Aiden suddenly crouched on top the golden ball and pounded away, using his vampyren strength to attempt to break the barrier. It wasn't working. He pointed his hands downward, unleashing the scorching fire of the fae. That had no effect either.

Aiden glanced to his left, most likely in response to someone else, before flying away. Pierce flew into view, the veins on his forehead bulging as he released his deadly pink lightning. The last time he had let loose such a barrage, he'd disintegrated Ben in Aeaea. His power thundered all around us, but the golden sphere held.

Icarian quickly shifted his hand to the right, and another cry of pain forced its way out of my raw throat. "I've almost got it."

What was he searching for, and how the heck was it a part of his plan B?

A gasp escaped my throat when I realized what it could be. Icarian's alternate plan to killing Mason and his brothers was collecting the Crests of the Five. That could only mean one thing. Somehow, some way, I housed one of the crests.

The golden orb shuddered, and Icarian glanced away for a moment before chuckling. "It seems the High Priests are giving it the old college try now, but they won't fare any better than their children." He reached deeper, shoving his arm inside me all the way up to his elbow.

The world went white from the pain, and even though my burning throat told me I was still screaming, I could no longer hear my own cries. I suddenly felt myself floating, as if my mind was leaving behind my body and the anguish that tore it apart from inside.

I didn't want to go. I wanted to stay with Mason. We had a life to live together. We were supposed to go to Europe before college started in the fall and then get married after we graduated. Then there were the kids we'd talked about. Mason hoped we'd have three boys who would all be just like him. That was a terrifying thought. I wouldn't survive three mini-Masons. But as my body became lighter than air, I realized none of that was going to happen.

At least not in this lifetime.

We were spell bound, and we'd find each other again in our next reincarnation. We'd be even stronger in the future than we were right now. That gave me some comfort, but not as much as I'd get from being in Mason's arms, feeling his breath fanning across my cheeks, inhaling the musky-sweet scent that made me want to devour him, and tasting the kisses that breathed life into my soul.

"I've got it." Icarian grasped something, and I could feel it, not in my flesh but in my soul.

Once he pulled it out of me, it would all be over. I would release my grip on this world and this life. But I couldn't go without saying what was in my heart one final time. "I love you, Mason."

"I love you too." Mason floated next to us, resting on a cloud of shadows that stretched wide across the sky. It was as if every shadow within a hundred miles had gathered here upon his command. He switched his gaze from me to Icarian, and his blue eyes turned harder than diamond. "Get your fucking hands off my boyfriend!"

Dozens of muscled, ebony arms extended from the inky nimbus around us and squeezed the golden sphere. The walls shook, and stress fractures cracked across the surface.

"How is this possible?" Icarian shuddered as Mason split the ball open like an eggshell.

Before Icarian could react, black spikes pierced his golden body. Crimson liquid trailed from the weapons as Icarian's hand slowly withdrew from my soul, leaving behind whatever object he'd been after. For a few moments, I floated in the air, but before I could plummet to my death, a black cloud came to rest underneath me and carried me to Mason's side.

My cloud merged with his, and a second later Mason held me in his arms. My exhausted body trembled upon contact, as if it knew what it needed to heal had finally arrived. From his touch alone, my injured soul drew strength, but it wasn't enough. I craved the one thing that would make it all better—Mason's kiss.

When he pressed his lips to mine, it was like a spring rainstorm unleashed within my soul, and I longed to lie naked under the downpour. The breath from his kisses filled my lungs with new life as if wave after wave of rejuvenating waters flooded my body and refreshed my soul. I trailed my tongue along his chin and neck, licking the salt from his body, and my previously numb flesh came to life with goose bumps that spread over every aching inch of my skin.

I had never tasted anything better or felt more alive.

Mason pulled out of our life-sustaining kiss and rested his forehead against mine. "Damn. That was like the best kiss ever."

That was an understatement. "Yes, it was."

"Are you okay?"

"I will be." I wrapped my arms around him before nuzzling into his neck. "Now."

"That was an unexpected development." Icarian floated above us.

Mason tensed around me as he pulled me tight against him. "How are you not dead?"

Icarian chuckled. "It'll take a bit more than this to bring about my end." While that might be true, the strain in his metallic voice told me Mason had inflicted major damage.

"Well, okay, then." With one sweeping gesture from Mason, the shadows that draped across the sky rose like a tidal wave. They crashed upon Icarian, swallowing his golden light beneath their inky folds. Arrows of light suddenly pierced the gloom, ripping giant holes in the murk.

Icarian flew through one of the openings, his golden body shaking with anger. "I haven't wanted to kill you. Don't force my hand." He pointed one glowing limb at where Mason and I stood, and a burst of golden light exploded forth.

Mason made an upward motion with his right hand. In response, the swirling, black clouds formed a solid barrier. An explosion shook the heavens as their magic collided. Mason's wall didn't fall. Instead, the shadows absorbed the light. "I can do this all day long."

"So I see." Icarian slowly descended toward us as he turned his glowing head to me. "What I have feared is coming true. Mason's power grows exponentially. Soon his brothers will follow. When all three of them wield the power of gods, all of creation will suffer."

Mason shifted his gaze from Icarian to me. "What the hell is he talking about?"

"Nothin'. He's ramblin' like a frightened old man."

"You will see, Drake Carpenter." Icarian floated upward, his light form glowing brighter the higher he traveled. "What will come could have been prevented today. Let's hope I can still stop it tomorrow."

Icarian spread his hands outward as he kissed the sky before exploding in golden brilliance. When the light faded, he was gone.

CHAPTER 15

MASON AND I descended on his cloud of shadows to cheers and applause. Everyone, even the scowling Edwells, seemed impressed by what Mason had accomplished. It was truly an astounding feat. Icarian possessed abilities that had taken out all of the protector covens, yet somehow Mason had been able to battle him to a standstill.

Was there some truth to Icarian's prophecy?

When our feet once again touched the earth, Mr. Blackmoor scooped Mason and me into his arms. After giving us both a squeeze and kissing the tops of our heads, he held us at arm's length and gave us his customary once-over. "Are you okay?"

"Yes, Dad. We're fine." Mason blushed. He hated when his father got emotional in front of everyone. It didn't bother me. It reminded me I was still a part of a loving family, something I would never take for granted again.

"I'm better, Mr. Blackmoor." I took Mason's hand in mine and squeezed it. "Thanks to Mason."

"Good." His grateful smile suddenly retreated before he smacked the both of us on the sides of our heads.

"Hey!" Mason rubbed himself and winced. "What was that for?"

"For disobeying a direct order." The other High Priests gathered behind him, their eyes slanted with disapproval. "I told you both to stay out of this. Instead you got yourselves kidnapped and almost killed. What the hell were you thinking?"

Mr. Stonewall snorted. "They weren't. As usual."

"Are you kidding me?" Mason pointed to the sky where he had battled Icarian. "I just beat the snot out of the bad guy."

The fury lines across Mr. Blackmoor's forehead grew deeper. "Something you wouldn't have had to do if you'd come to *me* about Drake's dream." The disappointment in his voice hurt more than Icarian's hand in my chest.

"That's my fault." I hung my head and took a step forward. "I kept it a secret because I wasn't sure what it all meant. I planned on tellin' you once I figured it out."

My apology did nothing to douse the flames in Mrs. Proctor's eyes. "And *that* was a mistake. You sought the help of my children instead of the High Priest of your coven. Do you realize how careless and foolish that was? Dream magic is not something to be trifled with. It is extremely difficult and can only be mastered by a truly powerful warlock, witch, or wizard. If Charlotte and Miranda hadn't told us about your dream or what they discovered about dream magic, we might never have found you. A simple scrying spell can't pierce the veil of such an incantation."

She was right. Even though I was immune to most magic, I didn't possess the knowledge of the other High Priests, Thad, or even Pierce. I had been reckless, and I had placed Charlotte and Miranda in an impossible situation. "I shouldn't have gone behind Mr. Blackmoor's back. It was careless and dangerous. We got way in over our heads, but hopefully what we've learned might make up for it."

That got the attention of the Stonewalls. As wizards, they believed information to be worth whatever risk necessary to obtain it. Mr. Stonewall fixed his gaze on me. "What did you learn?"

"We would be interested in hearing that as well."

As usual, the Conclave appeared after all the hard work was done. For some of the most powerful members of the magical community, they sure knew how to avoid a fight.

Gerald Wa lowered his hood and approached Mason and me. He cupped our cheeks and smiled. "It does my heart good to see you both well. When the protector covens contacted us about your abduction, I was beside myself with worry." Then he lightly slapped our faces. "Don't do that again."

While Mason grumbled about getting hit for the second time in under five minutes, I took the punishment and the warning with a smile. Even after everything involving Gerald and Aunt Millie's pendant, he was the only one on the Conclave I trusted to tell me the truth about what I'd learned.

"Now tell us. What have you discovered?"

I took a deep breath, and when I let it out, I told them about the kidnapping, being a witch hunter, and learning Mason and I were spell bound as enemies.

Pierce scratched his head. "I was unaware two souls could be spell bound by anything other than love."

"It's the rarest form of reincarnation," Mr. Stonewall admitted with a nod. "But the bond between the two souls is just as strong as those connected by love."

"And the relationship is far more turbulent." Mrs. Stonewall glanced between Mason and me, a curious expression playing across her face. "When two souls are spell bound by love, their destiny remains unchanged. They meet, they fall in love, they die, they are reborn, and the process begins anew. Souls bound by hate—"

"I do *not* hate Drake." Mason scowled at her comment.

"Of course not." Gerald patted Mason's back and motioned for Mrs. Stonewall to continue.

"Souls bound by a *different* emotion create unstable relationships that change with each rebirth. Their passion is often greater, overshadowing souls bound by love. When their relationship is good, the world is good. When it is not, when disaster strikes as it so often does in life, the churning passions that were once so wonderful can be disastrous."

"Drake? Is everything all right?" Gerald's kind, gray eyes hooded in concern. He'd apparently clued in to how that bit of information unnerved me, especially considering Icarian's fear. Would our relationship be responsible for bringing about the prophecy?

"I—"

"So let me get this straight." Mr. Edwell wobbled forward on his squat legs, his beady eyes trained on Mason and me. With a snort, he gave his back to my coven and addressed the Stonewalls, the Proctors, and the Conclave. "What you're saying is that we have yet one more reason to fear the instability of the Blackmoor coven?"

Mrs. Edwell nodded. "That's what I heard."

"Keep talking about my family." Mr. Blackmoor towered over Mr. Edwell, a growl forming in the back of his throat. "And I'll pound you like a nail into the ground."

That was the Warlock Hag's cue. She hovered protectively next to the Edwells, as if her favorite pets were about to be kicked in the head. Why did she love them so much and hate us just as strongly? "Here you are again, Oliver, threatening a member of another coven right in front of us." Why did she sound so pleased with herself? "*When* will you ever learn?"

Mr. Blackmoor hesitated as if something she said struck a chord in him, and he gazed deep into the folds of her hood.

"Enough!" Gerald stepped forward. "This bickering is getting us nowhere."

The others nodded in agreement.

When Gerald was satisfied the arguing had ceased, he turned back to me. "Is there more you haven't told us?"

There was—a lot more—but I wasn't sure how everyone was going to take it. "I don't think Icarian has the Air Crest."

Gasps set off all around me as the Warlock Hag settled her hooded gaze on me for the first time. "That's ridiculous. We already know Icarian stole the crown of the Beast King. The shifter told us this."

Kale shook his head. "That's not true. I only said it had been stolen from King Caspian. We have no proof it was Icarian." When he settled his golden gaze on me, the hope in his eyes was unmistakable. "Do you know where it is? Did Icarian say anything about its location?"

I would do anything to take the worry from my new friend's eyes, but I didn't have the information he desperately needed to hear. "I don't, but I'm certain it's not with Icarian."

The Warlock Hag snorted. "Why should we trust the word of a witch hunter?"

I winced and Mason almost came unglued. A shake of Gerald's head kept him quiet.

He gazed at his colleague and sighed. "There's no need for that. Drake has proven himself time and again as a friend to the magical community. What he is by birth shouldn't change our opinion of him."

"I disagree." She floated over to me. Even though I couldn't see her eyes, I could feel them boring into my soul. I stood my ground and didn't let her obvious hatred shake me. "His kind has sought to exterminate us for more than two millennia."

"That's funny. That's exactly what the witch hunters say about you."

She raised her hand, evidently ready to strike me dead, but suddenly Gerald stood between us. "That's enough."

Her only response was silence before she backed up and floated away.

Gerald grasped my hand and forced me to look at him. "Why do you think Icarian isn't in possession of the Air Crest?"

"Because he used the crests to get through my immunity to magic, and he only had the Earth and Fire Crests with him."

Gerald couldn't be any more surprised than if I picked him up and shook him like a rag doll. "Are you certain?"

"Whether he's certain or not, this means nothing." The Warlock Hag waved my words away. "He could have secured the Air Crest somewhere else."

"That wouldn't make any sense." This time Mr. Stonewall stepped forward. "If someone as powerful as Icarian has been collecting these talismans, the safest place for them to be is with him, especially if someone else is after them."

"Lawrence is correct." Gerald rubbed his chin in thought. "Yet another player is on the field, and it's someone we know absolutely nothing about."

That was exactly what I feared earlier. Someone else was after the crests, but who could that be?

A thought lodged in my brain like a butcher knife. Icarian had been the one who freed Ben from his prison, and only the Conclave knew of its location, just as the Conclave were the only ones who knew where all the crests, with the exception of the Spirit Crest, were located. If no one else knew that information, then Icarian and whoever else was after the crests most likely had to be *in* the Conclave.

"Are you okay?" Mason ran his hand up and down my back. "You look like you've seen a ghost."

No. I wasn't okay. If I was right, we were all in more danger than we believed.

"What is it?" Gerald asked. "Did you remember something else? If you do, please tell us. We need as much information as possible."

So did I. That was why I definitely wasn't going to admit my hunch about one of the crests being within me. That would be like painting a bull's-eye on my back, and I'd been used for target practice enough for one day. "I'm just kinda freaked out by all this."

Mason wrapped his arms around me. How did he always know exactly what I needed? "Me too. There is one thing I've been thinking about, something Icarian said that I didn't understand."

Gerald drew closer. "What is it?"

"He mentioned something about the growth of my powers and those of my brothers."

Pierce and Thad gaped at their father. "Us?"

The other protector covens traded curious glances while Mr. Blackmoor's face darkened in fury. He only ever got that angry when he was terribly afraid. "What did he say exactly?"

Mason scrunched up his lips as he tried to recall Icarian's words before turning to me. "I can't remember. Do you?"

All eyes were suddenly on me. If I revealed Icarian's prophecy, I could potentially hurt the Blackmoors even more. The other protector covens didn't trust them, and the Warlock Hag wasn't exactly their biggest fan. The information might send everyone over the edge and cause an outright war. Why did it feel like this was what Icarian wanted me to do?

"Drake?" Gerald's question told me I'd been silent long enough.

"Sorry. I'm just tryin' to remember. There was so much goin' on up there. He did mention somethin' about their powers, but I can't remember exactly what."

"You must." The Warlock Hag suddenly appeared in front of me. Her altered voice sounded strange, as if there was an emotion besides anger and condescension painting its tones. "We have long wondered about the surprising power growth of the Blackmoor brothers, and it has been a source of much debate. If there is a connection between Icarian and his plans, I must know."

First she spoke with almost genuine emotion, and now she was using first person instead of her standard royal *we*. What was going on with her? "Th-that's all I know. I swear."

For several moments she studied me from the shadowy depths of her hood. Her tense shoulders told me she didn't believe me, and if she could use her powers to pluck the information out of my brain, I had no doubt she would. I was more grateful for my immunity to magic than ever.

Gerald's voice suddenly broke the silence. "It seems we have much to ponder."

"Yes, we do." The Warlock Hag floated back to the line of robed figures, her hooded gaze remaining focused on me. "We will learn what we need to know, no matter what the cost."

I gulped. That sounded like a threat.

WHILE EVERYONE continued to speculate about the information I shared, I headed over to the witch hunters to say my final good-bye. The Conclave planned on wiping their memories and erasing their threat once and for all. Although I wasn't happy about the decision, it was for the best. Flint and his men would never stop gunning for us, and because of them, my cousin would forget I ever existed.

"And you're sure they won't be turned into vegetables?"

"No, they won't." Gerald walked with Mason and me across the field. As a favor, he promised to perform the spell that would wipe their minds. "I can cast the spell in such a way that only their knowledge about us and magic will be erased. They will then be returned to their lives prior to this, where they will hopefully be happy and where we will most certainly remain safe from them."

Mason squeezed my hand tight. He understood how hard this was for me. Even though I loved the family being with Mason provided me, Will was my blood. Allowing this to happen to him felt like a betrayal, and I wasn't sure how Will would take it.

"Drake!" Seeing us approach, Will rose from where he sat next to his silent, scowling father and jogged over. He flashed a smile at Mason before turning a wary eye to Gerald. "Hi. I'm Will, Drake's cousin." His cheery tone was like a knife in my chest.

Gerald extended his hand and returned the smile. "So I have heard."

After they shook in greeting, Will scrutinized Gerald's gray robes and hood. "Why are you dressed like a depressed monk?"

Mason snorted while I about died. Fortunately Gerald didn't take offense. I shuddered to think what would have happened to Will had he said that to the Warlock Hag.

"I do look like a depressed monk, don't I?"

Will gave him a single nod. "A little." His disdain for Gerald's wardrobe quickly disappeared when he turned his attention back to us. "And you two? What the fuck was up with that glowing disco ball you were fighting? I know you two are gay, but come on!"

Mason laughed, and it was genuine. He no longer scowled at the sight of Will, and it made me love him even more. "I don't know. You should see us go up against Hello Kitty sometime."

Will's chuckle lit up his expression, but another emotion crouched at the corners of his eyes. His darting gaze told me he was worried about what was going to happen next. He let out a long sigh and then dropped his gaze. "I'm real sorry about everything."

Mason punched his shoulder as if he were a straight boy hanging with his bro. "I know you are, but you've got nothing to apologize for. You didn't do this."

Will glanced over his shoulder at his father, whose gaze bored a hole through Mason's face. "But my dad did, and I want you to know that I had no fucking clue what he was up to. I know I'm a witch hunter and sh—" He darted his gaze to Gerald, no doubt realizing he was someone of great power and importance. "Well, I just want you all to know I'm not like them. I've seen what you guys can do. You could've killed all of us without breaking a sweat, but you didn't. That tells me you're good people."

"Thank you for that." Gerald's smile faltered as he no doubt reconsidered the decision that had already been made. "I wish there were more humans like you and Drake."

"Who doesn't?" Will's cheesy smile made us all laugh. He held out his fist to Mason. "So, we cool?"

Mason bumped the fist with his own. "Yeah."

"Are you two done jerking each other off?" Flint's rude comment earned him a sniff from Gerald and the snickers of his soldiers. "I know the old man there is just itching to get down to business."

Will shifted his gaze between the four of us, and suddenly I couldn't look him in the eyes. "What's he talking about?"

His father let fly a mocking snort. "We tried to kill them, and you *did* kill one of their kind a few hours ago. Do you really think they're just going to let us walk out of here?"

"But... I thought... I mean I didn't mean to...." Will sputtered, obviously feeling the need to defend himself. "She was trying to kill me and something inside me snapped. I didn't want to do it."

I understood what he was talking about because I had felt it too. It was the call of the witch hunter, and it was a difficult impulse to control when facing what we considered our natural enemy. My love for Mason gave me the strength I needed to overcome it, to keep from killing him when I had pulled the trigger in every other incarnation. Will didn't have that kind of connection to stop him from taking that witch's life. "We know that. It was a difficult spot to be in."

He glanced at Gerald. "Are you going to kill me?"

A reassuring smile spread across the old wizard's features. "No. That would break one of our cardinal laws, and that is a line I would never cross."

Will's suddenly relaxed posture communicated his relief.

"Tell him what you *are* going to do, old man." Flint locked gazes with Gerald and clenched his jaw. "I've heard stories about what you people to do us."

That tidbit instantly reknotted Will's muscles. "What's he going to do?"

Although Gerald had wanted to give Will the news, I had insisted I be the one to tell him. He was my cousin, and he deserved to hear it from me. "Gerald is goin' to take your memories so you're no longer a threat to us."

"Take my memories? What the hell does that mean?"

"It means he's going to erase your knowledge of magic, of being a witch hunter, of anything that might connect you to us."

"Why?"

"Because they know if they don't, we'll just come right back here and kill them all." The eagerness in Flint's tone revealed that was something he would definitely do if given the opportunity.

"Oh." Will stood silently for a moment. Sadness hooded his eyes, but he blinked it away. "So I won't remember you?

"No." My voice cracked, and the sob I'd been holding back slowly fought its way up my throat.

"And you're okay with that?"

"Of course not." I grabbed his shoulders and forced his eyes to mine. "We're family. If there was any other solution, believe me, I'd be all for it."

Will gazed far away into the distance, as if he was no longer here with me right now. "But you agree with their decision, then?"

My emotions seized control of my throat, so I nodded.

Will shrugged off my touch and backed away. "Dad was right. You are a traitor." A snarl that reminded me of his father twisted his expression into something ugly and hateful. "I was okay with you saving Mason. That made sense to me because you loved him, but this." He shook his head and glared at me. "This is choosing more than just Mason. This is choosing their safety, their well-being, over someone who is *actually* family."

"Will, please." Tears streamed down my face as Mason wrapped his arms around my chest and held me against him. This was what I feared, that my last memory of Will would be filled with anger and resentment. I didn't want that for him or for me. "I need you to understand."

He held up his hand and looked away. "You made your choice. Since I won't remember anything after today, you'll be the only one who has to live with it." He sat down next to his father, and no matter how much I begged him to hear me out, his eyes never met mine again.

I collapsed against Mason as Gerald began the spell that would wipe me from Will's mind. When it was done, Will, Flint, and all the soldiers fell into a deep sleep. A second later they were gone, returned to the lives they'd led before Havenbridge, lives that no longer included hatred of magic and no longer included me.

Will was right, I was going to have to find a way to live with this, but that wouldn't be today.

I'D NEVER been so grateful to see Blackmoor Manor in my life. It meant the nightmare was finally over. Well, at least for now, but I had no plans to dwell on that. All I wanted was to crawl into bed with Mason and escape the grief and fear that had eaten away at me the entire way back.

Fortunately Mason read me like a book. As soon as we crossed the threshold, he grabbed my hand and led me to our bedroom. He took off my clothes, escorted me to the shower, held me under the hot spray, and let me cry.

After toweling us both off, he guided me to our bed and we crawled under the sheets together. He pressed his naked body against mine and a kiss to the back of my neck. "Rest. I've got you."

And I knew he did, so I slept, and I dreamed about Will, about meeting him that first day in the cafeteria, about how much he enjoyed pissing off Mason, about how much he drooled after Miranda, and I laughed and I cried some more. Not once did Mason ever let me go.

We stayed in our room for the next few days, sometimes talking about what happened but most often just using the power of our touch to heal our wounds.

Mr. Blackmoor brought food and checked up on me at least three times a day. He also gave us the homework assignments he picked up at school so we wouldn't get too far behind. Although he gave me the space I needed to cope, he was still a father, looking out for my future. I loved him so much for that.

When I woke up on the fifth day of my self-imposed exile, the light streaking through the window didn't blind me or send me burrowing back into the covers or Mason's arms. I embraced the warmth that traveled up and down my naked flesh.

It rejuvenated me, melting the chill that had previously coated my skin like permafrost. The grief and fear that had coiled around me finally eased up, and though they didn't completely fall away, their hold over my aching heart would never again grip me as tightly as it had the past few days.

"Do you even know how beautiful you are when you smile?" Mason grinned over at me from his pillow. As always, his hair was a tangled mess because he didn't turn in his sleep, he flopped.

I scooted over to him, leaving the warmth of the sun for the heat of his loving gaze that sizzled more than my flesh. It set fire to my soul. Draping my right leg over his midsection, I snuggled close and sighed. "You only think that because you love me."

"I do." He pressed a kiss to my forehead and inhaled my scent. According to him, the way I smelled was even better than coffee. "Very much."

"I'm glad, because I don't know where I'd be right now if I didn't have you."

"You're strong, Drake. I don't think you realize how strong you are."

Although I felt better than I had in the past few days, I was a far cry from being strong. Right now an excited puppy could take me out. "Being immune to magic helps with that."

He readjusted our positions so we were lying side by side and face-to-face. "I'm not talking about that. Your strength doesn't come from your ability to cancel out magic. It comes from here." When he placed his hand over my chest, I shivered. It had been too long since his hands traveled my flesh, and my body craved for his hand to dip much lower.

"You've been through so much, and you never let it drag you down. You always get back up. I admire that about you."

"You admire me?" I crawled on top of him, resting my bare butt on his growing hardness before leaning over and pressing a kiss to his perfect lips.

"I'm in awe of you." His breath fanned across my skin as he explored my body with his hands, tracing his fingertips along my shoulders before dancing them down my spine. "You're always able to do what's right, what's good, no matter how much it hurts. You think about everyone else before you think about yourself. I know what happened with Will knocked the wind out of you for a while. Who wouldn't feel as if they'd been kicked in the nuts? But the fire is back in your eyes. You're ready to get out of this bed, leave this room and this house, and face whatever else is waiting for us out there. That's strength, and that's what makes you stronger than everyone in this house combined."

He was right. I was stronger than I gave myself credit for. I focused too much on what I'd lost instead of on how much I had gained through sheer persistence. While I was ready to start living my life again, I definitely wasn't leaving this bed just yet. I sat up, stroking Mason to full mast with one hand while tracing fluttering circles around his hardening nipples.

Mason groaned as he surfed his hands up and down my chest, trailed them over my stomach, and stroked my throbbing length. He swiped a finger over the drop of liquid at the slit before shoving it in his mouth and savoring my taste.

His eyes rolled back in his head. "Better than coffee."

I chuckled. Apparently everything about me was better than coffee, which brought a deliriously happy grin to my face. I wanted to be what Mason needed and desired because he was everything I craved.

I slipped my tongue between his lips and shared the sweetness my body produced. His excited moans and his tongue alive in my mouth dispelled the remaining gloom from the shadowy recesses of my soul. It couldn't stand the light Mason's touches and kisses sent streaking through me like golden arrows.

He kneaded my cheeks, squeezing them in frantic want as he thrust himself harder and faster into my grip.

"I've missed this," he panted.

Even though we hadn't been apart for the past few days, I missed his touch, his breath, his kisses. Our souls were bound throughout time by love, and it was time for our bodies to follow suit. "Please, Mason." I held his erection against me, sliding him between my crevice and open palm. "I need you inside me."

Mason didn't need my request repeated. He turned me over onto my back and settled between my legs. He pressed his body onto me, letting me feel the weight of his desire, and I wrapped my legs around his waist, grinding his hardness against mine.

He covered my chest with his mouth, licking delirious trails down the slope of my body before planting breathy kisses against my upper thigh and groin. I arched my back off the mattress when he swirled his tongue through the light dusting of hair and wrapped it around the base of my cock. While he gently massaged my full sac, he teasingly nibbled up the shaft, alternating between lapping at the hardened flesh and blowing puffs of air along the heated skin.

"Mason, please. I need you."

"And you'll have me. Soon." He kissed the head of my cock, lapping up the silky threads coating the head before taking me down his throat.

A cry of pleasure tore from my throat, and my entire world became singularly focused on the wet warmth enclosing me. The more of me Mason greedily consumed, the stronger and freer I became. I clutched at the sheets when he increased the suction and pace and paired that with long, circular strokes of my shaft with his hand.

I wanted him so badly that my body was already on the verge of climax.

I threw my head against the mattress and gripped his shoulders as Mason's mouth tore the orgasm from my body. When my spent cock slipped free of his lips, Mason covered my mouth with his. The taste of our joined fluids reignited the fire he'd just drained from my body, and I suddenly wanted more.

"Will you…?" I asked between ragged breaths. "Now?"

He grinned at me before reaching into the bedstand and bringing out a bottle of lubricant. "Yes."

As he lubed himself up, I grabbed the backs of my knees and pulled them to my chest, giving Mason the access he needed and that my body demanded he have. I felt so much more alive now, but I wasn't yet complete. Once Mason's body entered mine and he filled me with his love, then I would truly have want I needed to face the future.

Mason leaned over me, supporting his weight with one arm while aiming himself at my entrance with the other. "Are you ready?"

I'd never been more ready in my life. "Yes. Do it."

He pressed himself against me, his head rubbing against the muscled rim, and my body instantly relaxed, ready to receive the gift we only gave to each other. With gentle pressure, my body opened up as he entered. I clawed at his shoulders and his back as the full length of him slid inside me.

When he was buried to the hilt, he wrapped his arms around me, bringing our lips together as he began his slow, torturous strokes in and out of my flesh. We kissed deeply. His breath became mine and mine became his. We were no longer Mason and Drake. We were one in body and in soul, and I clung to that feeling, savoring the delicious fullness Mason drove into me. Every thrust, every push reminded me I wasn't alone, that I'd never be alone, that he would be by my side and in me for the rest of my life.

Sweat fell off Mason's body like rain, creating a heavy cloud of sex and musk that filled my lungs. The scent and his relentless thrusting hips moving in long, circular motions, brought me right back to the precipice I'd previously fallen over, and I opened my arms wide, preparing for the inevitable plunge we would take together.

"Drake." My name came from his mouth in a low grumble. He was close and so was I. I reached between our sweat-slick bodies, taking myself in hand. With a final thrust, Mason tensed for one glorious moment as he rode the high we created before my body brought him to a trembling climax.

As Mason spilled himself inside me, the pulsing waves of his dick began the ripples of my second orgasm. I stroked myself faster until I exploded onto our sweat-soaked bodies.

"Wow!" Mason crumpled on top of me, spent, and I held him close. I stroked the back of his neck while my legs remained wrapped around his waist. I wanted him inside me for as long as he was able.

"Tell me about it."

After a few minutes, Mason's retreating length slipped free, and though the fullness in my body was gone, my soul had never been more satiated.

"I don't know what it was." Mason fell onto the mattress and pulled me onto his chest. He gazed up at me, moving my sweaty blond locks out from my vision. "But that time was different."

I'd felt it too. Some unseen door in the both of us had been unlocked. Whatever Mason and I had created when we first got together had fully formed. It was now ready to take on reality. "It was wonderful."

"So." He nodded to the locked bedroom door. "Do you think you're ready to head back into the world?"

I was. We had a lot to accomplish. I still had to tell Mason and the family about the Prophecy of the Three, and we had to stop Icarian and the Spell Fall. A lot of unknowns waited for us in the shadows, but they no longer frightened me. No matter what, Mason and I had each other's back, not as two enemies bound by hate, but as two young men bound by the choice of love. Icarian, the prophecy, and the Spell Fall didn't stand a chance.

I gazed down into his gorgeous blue eyes and gave him the devilish smirk he often gave me. "The more important question is: Do you think the world is ready for us?"

For bonus content from

THE WARLOCK

BROTHERS OF

HAVENBRIDGE

check out

www.havenbridge.me

JACOB Z. FLORES lives a double life. During the day, he is a respected college English professor and midlevel administrator. At night and during his summer vacation, he loosens the tie and tosses aside the trendy sports coat to write man-on-man fiction, where the hardass assessor of freshmen-level composition turns his attention to the firm posteriors and other rigid appendages of the characters in his fictional world.

Summers in Provincetown, Massachusetts, provide Jacob with inspiration for his fiction. The abundance of barely clothed man flesh and daily debauchery stimulates his personal muse. When he isn't stroking the keyboard, Jacob spends time with his daughter. They both represent a bright blue blip in an otherwise predominantly red swath in south Texas.

Blog: jacobzflores.com
Facebook: www.facebook.com/jacob.flores2
Twitter: @JacobZFlores
Pinterest: www.pinterest.com/jacobflores2
Goodreads: www.goodreads.com/author/show/5142501.Jacob_Z_Flores
Google Plus: plus.google.com/u/0/+JacobFlores9595/posts

JACOB Z. FLORES

SPELL BOUND

THE WARLOCK BROTHERS OF HAVENBRIDGE: BOOK ONE

The Warlock Brothers of Havenbridge: Book One

Mason Blackmoor just can't compete with his brothers, much less his father. They represent the epitome of black magic, strong, dark, and wicked, and though Mason tries to live up to his respected lineage, most of the spells he casts go awry. To make matters worse, his active power has yet to kick in. While his brothers wield lightning and harness the cold, Mason sits on the sidelines, waiting for the moment when he can finally enter the magical game.

When a dead body is discovered on the football field of his high school, Mason meets Drake Carpenter, the new kid in town. Drake's confident demeanor and quick wit rub Mason the wrong way. Drake is far too self-assured for someone without an ounce of magical blood in his body, and Mason aims to teach him a lesson—like turn him into a roach. And if he's lucky, maybe this time Mason won't be the one turned into an insect.

Not surprisingly, the dislike is mutual, and Drake does nothing to dispel Mason's suspicion that the sexy boy with a southern drawl is somehow connected to the murder.

If only Mason didn't find himself inexplicably spell bound whenever they are together, they might actually find out what danger hides in the shadows.

www.dreamspinnerpress.com

JACOB Z. FLORES

BLOOD
TIED

THE WARLOCK BROTHERS OF HAVENBRIDGE: BOOK TWO

The Warlock Brothers of Havenbridge: Book Two

Thad Blackmoor's heart is as cold as his icy magical abilities. He considers emotions a waste of his time and prefers to study the arcane, using the sacred books of his coven to grow in his craft. He aspires to supersede his father and elder brother Pierce in power, and now that his younger brother, Mason, has tapped into the rare warlock power of darkness, he needs to work harder than ever.

But Thad's ambitions are halted when he saves Aiden Teine, a fire fairy, from a banshee. Thad's immediate attraction to Aiden catches him off guard and thaws his cold heart for the first time. As Thad, Aiden, and his brothers investigate the connection between the banshee attack and the vampyre and shadow weaver who almost killed them, Thad tries to dodge Ben, a sexy warlock who won't let him be after a one-night stand.

Their search for answers leads them to the Otherworld, where something even more insidious is at work—something Thad will need more than logic to stand against.

www.dreamspinnerpress.com

JACOB Z. FLORES

SOUL STRUCK

THE WARLOCK BROTHERS OF HAVENBRIDGE: BOOK THREE

The Warlock Brothers of Havenbridge: Book Three

Like the electricity he commands, Pierce Blackmoor streaks through life on raw power and pure sexual energy. His conquests on the battlefield and in the bedroom form his foundation, but that bedrock crumbles when his younger brothers' abilities surpass his own. Pierce finds himself at an all-time low, and clawing his way back to the top becomes his only concern.

Pierce's plan to reassert his dominance, however, takes a backseat when he wounds Kale Aquilo, an emissary of the Beast King, lord of all shifters.

Kale's beguiling nature shoots like a lightning bolt straight to Pierce's soul, and when the soft-spoken Kale relays that a virus is killing his people, Pierce abandons his quest for power to do something he has never done before—protect someone other than himself.

As Kale, Pierce, and his brothers struggle to find the root of the magical virus spreading plague across Aeaea, the shifter island, they face a gauntlet of old and new foes. Soul struck, Pierce and Kale must uncover the truth behind the conspiracy gathering in the shadows.

www.dreamspinnerpress.com

JACOB Z. FLORES

Please
REMEMBER
Me

Successful lawyer Santi Herrera couldn't be happier with the direction his life is taking. Not only is he on track to becoming a partner in his law firm, but he's planning his wedding to Hank Burton, a south Texas contractor who has made a name for himself despite his humble beginnings. The introverted lone wolf Santi and the friendly, outgoing Hank complement each other perfectly. From the moment they laid eyes on each other, they were hooked, and as far as Santi and Hank are concerned, a happily ever after is their destiny.

But fate deals them a devastating new hand.

A construction accident leaves Hank with severe head trauma and brings him precariously close to death. When he finally awakens, Hank doesn't remember Santi or the love they shared for the past three years. Santi faces the greatest challenge of his life. Can he respark a flame his lover can't recall? And can he stop the diverging paths that fickle fate charts between them?

Santi has faith in the love he and Hank shared and in the words his father once spoke to him: "It's never too late to fall in love. All over again."

www.dreamspinnerpress.com

DREAMSPUN DESIRES

UNDERCOVER BOYFRIEND

Jacob Z. Flores

One Fine Day

*Two men, one lie, and
a whole bunch of trouble.*

A One Fine Day Novel

Two men, one lie, and a whole bunch of trouble.

Marty Valdez is in serious trouble. His sister's wedding is around the corner, and everyone expects to meet Marty's super-successful underwear model boyfriend—whom Marty invented. Now Marty has to produce a half-naked hottie or suffer the worst humiliation of his life.

FBI agent Luke Myers is in serious trouble. He's been working undercover to take down a dangerous drug cartel, but his cover's blown and he needs to disappear. Luckily, a geeky yet intriguing comic book artist gives him the perfect opportunity. Luke just has to pretend to be his boyfriend, and pretending is what he does best. But between Marty's mother and his ex, Luke might've bitten off more than he can chew, and Marty's knack for finding trouble might ruin more than just his sister's wedding.

www.dreamspinnerpress.com

www.ingramcontent.com/pod-product-compliance
Lightning Source LLC
Chambersburg PA
CBHW060102260626
47160CB00005B/1763